Ideal Marriage

a novel by

Peter Friedman

The Permanent Press
Sag Harbor, New York, 11963

Copyright© 2004 by Peter Friedman

Library of Congress Cataloging-in-Publication Data

Friedman, Peter, 1936-
    Ideal marriage : a novel / by Peter Friedman.
      p. cm.
    ISBN 1-57962-100-7 (alk. paper)
    1. Teenage boys--Fiction. 2. Sex customs--Fiction. I. Title.

    PS3606.R57I24 2004
    813'.6—dc22

                        2003065547

Printed in The United States of America

THE PERMANENT PRESS
4170 Noyac Road
Sag Harbor, NY 11963

For Isabelle

Chapter One

THE LUXURY LINER

Et parce que tous les jours je t'aime davantage
Aujourd'hui plus que hier et bien moins que demain
And because every day I love you more. Today more than yesterday and much less than tomorrow.
Th. H. Van de Velde, M.D., *Ideal Marriage: Its Physiology And Technique*, quoting Rosemonde Gérard.

IT WAS SEPTEMBER 1957. I was sixteen, a junior in high school, and contemplating becoming a gigolo, just for a summer or two in Rome. Unlike the gigolos I had seen there in movies, I would be kind to the middle-aged women who kept me. I would be grateful to them, not only for the money I was earning, but for whatever I learned from them that I might later apply with my own wife. And I wouldn't ask for outlandish payment: merely enough to cover my trips, provide a little spending money for college, and above all, add to my savings account for my eventual marriage.

I took down my stamp album and laid it on the floor of my room. We lived in New York, at 75th Street and Madison Avenue on the 8th floor of a 12-story building.

Using Scott's stamp catalogue, I began valuing my collection. I wanted to see how much I could get for it, in case the gigolo business developed slowly or didn't work out. For hours, I pored over my stamps. Some of them I soaked in the sink to check for watermarks; others I examined with a magnifying glass for the faded surcharges of occupying countries. The value of a stamp sometimes turned on its exact color and tint: was it carmine ór scarlet, lake or vermilion? Depending on the answer, it might be worth anywhere from 3 or 11 cents up to $10.57—a difference that could give me two extra nights in Italy, or add that much more to my marriage fund. In cases of doubt, I assumed the lower valuation, to assure only pleasant surprises.

I had recently discovered the book, *Ideal Marriage: Its Physiology and Technique*, written in 1926 by a Dutch gynecologist, Th. H. Van de Velde. I found it late one night, hidden on my parents' hall bookshelf behind four volumes of the Yearbook of Agriculture. Intrigued, I tucked *Ideal Marriage* under my shirt on the left side—the side away from my parents' bedroom, in case one of them came out—and tiptoed to my room and closed the door.

Sitting on my couch, I ran a hand over the book's faded, pebbled green cover. How innocent it looked and felt, like just another textbook. If I hadn't noticed that it was hidden, I might never have picked it up. Why had my parents hidden the book? I wondered. What juicy things didn't they want me to read?

I scanned the table of contents: "Vigorous and Harmonious Sex Life," "Love Play," "Significance of Internal and External Secretions in Determining Approach." And on the list went, from "Sexual Perfumes," to "Penile Angle"; from "Erotic Zones" and "Bodily Manipulations and Caresses" to the "Special Significance of the Breast and Nipples," and three chapters on "Sexual Intercourse."

I coiled my fingers around, as if already caressing girls in the most stimulating ways, driving them wild with desire. The image aroused me, too.

Ideal Marriage wasn't erotically written. Nor did it contain any arousing pictures—only a few multi-colored diagrams of the male and female genitalia and their surrounding regions, looking like a confusing mixture of socks, tangled-up fishing lines, two hot water bottles, and an angry Raggedy Ann doll.

But I was thrilled by the book's opening promise—"I show you here the way to Ideal Marriage." Reading it, I knew that I'd found my life's goal, to have my own ideal marriage someday. I felt tears of happiness coming.

It all seemed clear. Surely nothing would ever be more important to me than to be married to someone I loved and who loved me back, the person with whom I'd be spending most of my life. The "husband as permanent lover of his wife," said *Ideal Marriage*. What a wonderful idea! While I'd no one in mind yet as a future wife, I wanted to begin preparing for marriage early, to get a head start.

I liked consulting the same marriage manual as my parents had used. Reading it, I felt linked with them across time, even to before I was born. I tried to picture them in their early twenties, poring over *Ideal Marriage*'s instructions on erotic caressing, then retiring to their bedroom to put them into practice. Imagining my parents as back in their twenties made it easier for me to picture them in bed together—as if they were different persons then, persons I had seen only in photographs.

Once I had finished reading *Ideal Marriage*, I'd move on to more modern works. It was like with photography, I thought, where I had first learned all I could with my Voigtländer folding camera, before trading it in for a Rolleicord.

On a Saturday in mid-September, I went out with a classmate, Eleanor Fay, although she was my fourth choice among the girls at school. My first three choices were all dating other boys, and I thought that my training for marriage shouldn't be restricted to learning from books.

I picked Eleanor up at her apartment on 83rd Street and Riverside Drive. I was a little annoyed that she lived so far west, since the 79th Street crosstown bus stopped a long block earlier. In winter it would be cold, with the wind blowing off the Hudson River.

"We're glad Eleanor's going out with a nice boy like you,"

said her mother, as she and her husband greeted me. "Please remember me to your mother."

"I will, Missus Faye," I said, unsure whether I liked the "nice boy" part.

Eleanor was about five foot, seven inches, with dark hair and large features. She wore a scoop-necked black dress, with short, puffy sleeves, and a black ribbon around her throat. Although her lipstick was on thick and her pores glistened through her powder in a bright light, when all dressed up she looked okay.

I took her to see the movie, *Love in the Afternoon*, with Audrey Hepburn, on whom I had developed a crush in *Roman Holiday*.

Sitting in the darkened theater, I put my right arm around Eleanor's shoulders. Then I let my fingers explore a little, caressing her arm and moving down under it along her ribs, feeling the sudden softness where a breast began. For a while, I played along the frontier between her ribs and breast, intrigued by the contrast—the hard flesh on one side, soft on the other. Then feeling emboldened, I put my hand on her breast directly, all of this, of course, on the outside of her dress and bra. Eleanor nestled in closer to me. Her breathing grew louder and I felt myself growing excited.

I withdrew my hand and put it back around her shoulders. I realized that I didn't want to take Eleanor out again. But to go on touching her breasts, even just one breast, and then not ask her out again seemed hurtful. She might think that all I'd been interested in was feeling her up, which could have been true. Then for the next two years I would have to see her in class every day, looking hurt and angry at me. I hoped it wasn't already too late.

After the movie, I invited Eleanor to a Howard Johnson's for ice cream sodas. The counterman first filled a tall glass with syrup, milk, and seltzer, and then hooked a large scoop of ice cream onto the rim so it wouldn't fall into the glass and make the soda run over. I liked it that I was getting more in total this way. Most places put the ice cream *inside* the glass, leaving less room for the liquid.

"What proves the Soviet Union's a democracy," said Eleanor, "is that they fought against Germany in the war. If Stalin was a dictator, he would have been on Hitler's side."

"You're wrong," I wanted to say. "Russia fought Germany only because Hitler invaded them. Until then they had been allies."

If we had been in school, I probably would have argued with Eleanor. But out on a date, I felt that a higher standard was called for: looking for areas of agreement, instead of disagreement.

"You have an interesting point," I said, something my mother said when she disagreed, but didn't want to argue. I would have liked to add, "I think you're intelligent, but misguided," a favorite phrase of my father's, but I feared Eleanor might take it poorly.

"I'm so proud of my cousin!" she declared. "He's only nine and he's come out in favor of disarmament."

"Oh, really?" I said, wondering if I was too superficial, because I preferred concentrating on my ice cream soda to discussing politics with Eleanor.

"Would you like to come in?" she asked later, at the door of her family's apartment

I looked at my watch. Fortunately, it was after 11:30.

"Thank you, but I have to get back," I lied. "I'm way behind on my homework for Monday."

I felt myself in a dilemma. If I simply shook hands with Eleanor and didn't kiss her good-night, after what I had done at the movie, she would take it as a brush-off. But if I kissed her strongly, it would imply I was going to ask her out again. What I wanted was to give her a brief, transitional kiss, fulfilling my obligation from earlier, without creating new ones for the future.

"Good night," I said, then kissed her lightly. But she glued her lips to mine and held me. Her kiss felt soggy, and when she stuck her tongue into my mouth, I recalled the doctor's tongue depressor and how I had learned to breathe evenly around it, to avoid gagging.

I finally pulled away, said "sleep well," then walked off before Eleanor could kiss me again.

"Thank you for a nice evening," she called out. "I enjoyed it."

"You're very welcome," I called back, continuing towards the elevator.

When I got home, I saw that no light was showing from either my sister's or my parents' room.

"Sleep well, slightly lumpy Alice," I said quietly at my sister's door. She was 13½ and had entered puberty, but had not yet come out the other end. She looked as if her individual parts didn't quite fit together. While her breasts had developed, her legs were still scrawny and tubular, her skin had no sheen to it, and her rear end was thick. She wore blue or red ribbons in her dark hair. Her face was cute but babyish. She looked deceptively innocent, I thought, hiding her annoying unreasonableness.

"Bad character!" I said, shaking my finger at her door.

From Alice's room, I moved to my parents' doorway and gently tried their door. I found it locked.

I was doing a study, estimating my parents' frequency of intercourse by how often their door was locked. I would compare my findings with the Kinsey Reports' statistics for married men and women of my parents' ages and education. My father was 42 and a veterinarian; my mother, 39 and a school teacher. I considered the nature of their sex life important in evaluating the quality of their marriage. *Ideal Marriage* called "a vigorous and harmonious sex life" one of the four cornerstones "of the temple of love and happiness in marriage."

While getting ready for bed, I asked myself what lessons I could draw from my date with Eleanor. I decided to try an experiment. I took out four undershirts from my bureau and rolled them up, two by two, to simulate Eleanor's breasts (which I considered her best feature) and stuffed them inside my pillowcase, between it and the pillow. Then I lay down

10

without my pajama top on, holding the pillow against my chest, as if holding Eleanor. Her "breasts" felt good against my bare skin. Yet, I also realized, proud of my values, that breasts were relatively unimportant to me. I ranked them a distant fourth, behind a girl's face, personality, and legs. Only if the sum of all of the other qualities, mental and physical, of two girls was equal, might their breasts become decisive for me, like the Vice President's tie-breaking vote in the Senate.

I awoke the next morning to my recurrent fear that the Russians were about to bomb Wall Street. "We'll bury you!" Khrushchev had threatened America, and I still feared an attack coming at any moment. Even low-flying planes often sounded to me like bombs whining downward to explode, and the air-raid sirens turned on regularly at noon seemed to invite an attack then, when everyone would assume it was only a test.

Going to my window, looking south, I tried to figure out how strongly the shock wave and blast of a hydrogen bomb would reach me at 75th Street and Madison, on the eighth floor, taking into account all of the intervening buildings taller than eight stories, which I had repeatedly tried to estimate. I felt envious of my sister, whose room was to the north of my room and my parents'. If a hydrogen bomb hit Wall Street, we would go first and she might survive.

Even if the shock wave and blast didn't kill me, wouldn't the radiation? I looked at my hands and pictured them charring, and I imagined myself afraid even to look in a mirror and see my face burned, as well.

I always read *Ideal Marriage* in secret and then returned it to its hiding place afterwards, lest my parents take it away, saying I was too young for it. "We think it's something you'll appreciate more when you're older, dear," my mother would say. My father would tell me to concentrate on my schoolwork, and "forget about marriage until later. Preferably, much later." Nor did I tell Alice I was reading the book, in case she inadvertently let on to my parents, or intentionally told them when she was angry at me.

"Love," said *Ideal Marriage*, quoting Stendahl, "means taking pleasure in seeing, touching, perceiving with every sense, and in the closest possible contact, someone whom we find lovely and who loves us."

My parents' friends Chuck and Sue Finlay had been married for over twenty years, but I noticed them still touching each other continually. They radiated happiness. At meals, they held hands under the table and he stroked her arm. When helping Sue on or off with her coat, Chuck lingered and kissed her neck. Looking at them, I felt filled with hope for my own future. They had shown me what was possible.

I vowed that my wife and I would never adopt the custom of separating couples at dinner parties. Instead, we would sit together at meals and, like Chuck and Sue, caress each other under the table.

I thought about the contrast with my own parents. They kissed each other as if kissing a friend—a quick touch on the lips, like the repelling poles of a magnet. Yet, unlike some other couples I had seen, my parents were generally considerate of each other and never fought or got drunk in public. "I've always believed," my mother said to me, "that people should be able to wait and discuss their differences in private." All in all, I rated their marriage "above average."

One Friday I was having dinner at my second-best friend, Ken Kirschenbaum's house. Ken and I shared an interest in fly fishing and in watching sports on TV. During professional wrestling matches, we yelled at the ref for missing obvious fouls—the bad guy stepping on the good guy's face when he was down on the mat, or concealing a bar of soap in his trunks and rubbing it in the good guy's eyes. During hockey matches, we felt frustrated when a commercial ran on after play had resumed and we missed seeing a goal scored or a penalty committed.

I admired Ken's laid-back ways. He played folk and country guitar, with a twinkling smile accompanying lyrics of love's desolation, often interrupting his strumming to kiss his girlfriend of the moment, then pick right up on the next chord.

Over the consommé that evening, Ken's father berated his wife for starting in on a new sheet of postage stamps before finishing the old sheet.

"What does it matter?" she said. "Stamps are stamps. They all cost the same three cents."

"Because," said her husband, "I made a point of telling you I wanted you to finish the old sheet first. It's a matter of discipline, of doing things in the right order." His fingers rapped the table as his voice rose. "You deliberately ignored my request, didn't you?" He stood up. "I can't live this way. I'm going out for a sandwich."

Ken, his mother, and I finished dinner by ourselves. His mother tried to make conversation, but gave it up when, each time, her voice cracked and her eyes watered.

"It's not your fault, Mom," Ken said to her. "You know Pop and discipline."

I thought I should say something, too. I felt it was wrong of me just to go on eating, as if oblivious, while Ken's mother was miserable. I wanted to tell her she was right about the stamps— it didn't matter which sheet they came from—but I feared that my alluding to her quarrel with her husband might embarrass more than please her.

Instead, I said, "Mrs. Kirschenbaum, that's an interesting necklace you're wearing."

"Why, thank you, Andre," she said. "It's Zuni."

"Oh!" I said, wondering whether its being Zuni should mean something to me. "Well, it's very nice." Actually, I thought the necklace looked like a string of candied corn or of dyed teeth, but I felt glad to have complimented Ken's mother, to have made the effort. Now I could relax and enjoy my floating island for dessert.

I left soon after dinner, sensing that to linger on would be awkward for Ken and his mother, though I also wished I could observe what would happen when Ken's father returned.

I imagined my own wife apologizing to me for starting in on a new role of stamps before finishing the old. "Don't be silly,

13

darling," I would say to her. "Of course, you can use stamps in any order you want." I would kiss her to reassure her.

Another time, my parents and I had been invited out by the Thompsons for a lobster dinner on an evening when my sister had a sleepover date at a friend's. Willis Thompson, a friend and financial advisor of both my father and grandfather, was sixty-three and had recently married his third wife, Ronda, forty-two and voluptuous in a low-cut dress.

Ronda drank three scotches before dinner, while the other adults had one cocktail apiece, and I had a glass of ginger ale.

"Sweetheart, don't you think you've had enough?" Willis said to Ronda, as she waggled her glass at a waiter for another refill. "Everyone else is ready to order."

"Are you saying I'm stewed?" asked Ronda. "Is that what you're saying?"

"No, sweetheart. I'm only suggesting—"

"Oh, stop suggesting! Prissy little man. Don't you know, a gentleman doesn't count how many drinks a lady is having?"

"Please excuse Ronda. She had a few at home already." Willis smiled at the rest of us.

"That's right—tell everyone," said Ronda. "You think it's fun living with you? A whole week we don't go out, because he's taking care of his poor poor sore throat. Who wouldn't have a few? And that's not all I want a few of, is it, *sweetheart*?"

Willis turned to my father. "As I was suggesting, Ernest, I think you should get into discounted railroad bonds. You're bound to do well in a reorganization. The government will never let the railroads go under."

Ronda ordered a fifth scotch with dinner. Suddenly, I noticed her staring at me. I turned away, embarrassed. I realized I had been looking at the top of her décolletage, where an emerald pendant hung between her breasts. I had been comparing the softness of a breast with that of the lobster meat deepest within a claw. That deep claw meat seemed suspiciously soft to me, as

14

if, like a breast, it was made up of fat and tissue. I hesitated to eat it.

"What's the matter," Ronda asked me, "haven't you seen a lady high before?"

I looked back at her again.

"I'm not drunk, Andre, I'm *high*. "You know the difference?" She laughed. "My husband doesn't know. He married a luxury liner, but he won't let her out of dry dock." She lowered her voice and swayed toward me. "Come visit me, Andre. We'll have a good time. Just you and me, sweetie." She kissed her fingers and touched them to my face.

"That's it, Ronda, we're going home!" Willis stood up and dragged her toward the door, pulling with both hands, while she stuck out her tongue at him. "Ernest, please be so good as to settle the bill," he called back to my father. "I'll send you a check for it."

"That poor schnook!" said my father, after the Thompsons had gone. "At his age, you'd think Willis would have more sense than to marry such a floozy."

"I'm sure Ronda has qualities we're unaware of," said my mother. "She certainly looks striking."

"You would find virtues in Stalin. 'The Little Father had qualities that his people were unaware of,' you'd say. 'He was genuinely concerned about over-population in the twenty-first century.' No, Willis married Ronda because he was scared to live alone, poor devil. Now he's paying the price. If I had known, I would have said to him, 'Willis, have an affair with her instead.' Marrying Ronda not five months after Lucille died—it's indecent! Speaking of *indecency*, will anyone join me in a piece of cheesecake?"

I wondered whether you could properly say, "speaking of indecency," when you were the one who had spoken of it.

I thought about Ronda's invitation. ("Come visit me, Andre. I promise we'll have a good time.") Even with her drunk, losing my virginity would be wonderful, having it over with just like that. Then never again would I lack self-confidence. And whenever I got married, I would know that it would

15

be not just for sex, but out of love.

Actually, Ronda's being drunk could help me. She might overlook my inexperience.

My sleeping with her would be good for Ronda, too, I reasoned. I would do everything to satisfy her—whatever she wanted—all those little erotic touches described in *Ideal Marriage*, which Willis had surely forgotten or never learned, like the "tapotement," a light, elastic tapping on the loins and pelvic region. I pictured Ronda opening her blouse for me, button by button. Then unzipping her skirt and stepping out of it, and leading me by the hand into bed with her.... Just imagining it was too exciting. I had to calm myself down before standing up to leave the restaurant. My father was already paying the check.

I surreptitiously passed my hand over my lap, like a magician, commanding my penis to de-levitate, waving it down, as in doing the rising-and-falling-matchbox trick.

If only Ronda would phone me to repeat her invitation, I thought the next day. Then I would know she had meant it, that she hadn't forgotten when sober.

But maybe she was waiting for me to take the lead and call first. I would have to find a time when neither Alice nor my parents were around, and when it was unlikely that Willis would be home at Ronda's end. If I telephoned Ronda, what would I say?

"Hello, Mrs. Thompson? This is Andre. Andre Schulman, Ernest and Karen's son?... Oh, I'm fine, thank you, and yourself?....Good.....Well, I just wondered how you are?....(No, that wouldn't do—Ronda might think I was referring to her having been drunk at the dinner.) "I just wanted to tell you, I really enjoyed meeting you last Friday." (Wasn't that too forward—calling a married woman to say I had enjoyed meeting her?) "I really enjoyed seeing you and Willis last night." (That would be worse, reminding her that she was married, or implying that I had enjoyed seeing Willis as much as *her*.) Why not be direct: "You suggested I call you." (That would let Ronda know immediately that I was responding to her invitation.) Then, if she had forgotten or had changed her mind, she could always say something like, "I honestly can't remember why I'd asked you to call me. But it's nice of you to get in touch. Give my regards to your parents."

I imagined Ronda saying, instead, "Andre, I'm glad you called. I promised you a good time, didn't I? Well, Ronda is one lady who keeps her promises. When can you come over and collect?"

Each time I started to call, I felt embarrassed and my fingers slipped in the dialing holes. I put down the phone. Maybe Ronda would think me too childish for her, once the alcohol had worn off: "Who does this kid think I am?"

I stood up and went to my bathroom mirror, aware that I was stalling.

"You look very handsome," I said to myself, hearing my mother's voice. But I could see that my handsomeness—my blue eyes, sandy hair, and lean, five foot, eleven inch frame—was only superficial. My Adam's apple was too large and twitchy, and my face too babyish. It was almost characterless, like a child's drawing of a face. In snapshots I thought I looked retarded.

I finally decided to give Ronda the chance to call first. After all, *she* was the married one. I didn't want to feel responsible for coming between her and Willis. But if Ronda took the lead, that would be a different story. If she was going to commit adultery anyway, why not with me?

She never called. One day my father mentioned that the Thompsons were getting a divorce and that Ronda had gone to Reno for it. My parents remained loyal to Willis, calling him "the wronged party." I regretted their choice. I thought the "wronged party" the less interesting.

I regretted even more my cowardice in not having called Ronda before she left. I thought of Robert Frost's poem, "Two roads diverged in a yellow wood/ ... and I took the one less traveled by." What if I'd taken the road of calling Ronda and had wound up sleeping with her? As with Frost's traveler, that might have "made all the difference" for me, too. It would even have helped my plan of working summers as a gigolo to earn money for my eventual marriage. Surely I could serve my clients better if I'd already lost my virginity.

Chapter Two

PARENTAL STUDIES

"Love ... can permanently bless both
partners. It *can* do so; but how often do the
fairest feelings fade, the most solemn
intentions subside!

Ideal Marriage, p. 18.

ON A SUNDAY in late September, I was walking along
Madison Avenue with my parents. They were planning to go
into Central Park at 72nd Street and Fifth Avenue to look at the
early fall foliage. I decided to walk with them until the park. I
knew I wouldn't feel relaxed inside, looking at the foliage with
my father along. He would keep quizzing me on the names of
the trees.

The only two trees I felt sure of were the paper birch, with
its thin, white, peelable bark, and the maple, whose leaves I recognized from the uniforms of the Toronto Maple Leafs hockey
team. The other trees all ran together in my mind—elm and oak,
cedar and chestnut, hemlock and hickory. I wished they had just
remained street names, without being attached to trees as well.

Walking with my parents, I felt like a diplomat. I kept trying to bring them closer together. My father strode ahead, my
mother lagged behind, and I walked alone in the middle, wanting to side with neither. Or I hurried back and forth between
them, trying to speed up my mother and slow down my father.

"Shall we wait for Mom?" I said, when my father and I had
reached a street corner, while my mother was still a half block

behind.

"Of course!" my father agreed. But when the traffic light turned green and then red again and my mother had made little progress, he called out, "Karen dear, if you hurry, we can make the next light."

I ran back to my mother, who was looking in a dress shop window. "Mom, you *know* how Dad feels about missing two lights in a row."

"Tell him to go on ahead," she said. "I'll catch up later. I like looking in store windows. Your father likes counting traffic lights. We're each doing what we want."

I dashed up to my father to tell him, then ambled back down the block to a camera store. In the window was a Rolleicord, like the one I had recently bought on a trade-in at my grandfather's photo store. When I looked down into the Rolleicord's reflex-mirror viewfinder, the most ordinary scenes became magical—my room, the traffic on the street, my parents and sister at dinner. And the Rollei's square format let me catch subjects unawares. I could seem to be looking in one direction, while actually photographing off at a 90-degree angle, perfect for a shy guy like myself.

"Andre," said my mother, coming up to me, "if you hurry, we can make the next light."

I told myself that studying my parents' marriage offered me another way of preparing for my own. "Those who cannot remember the past are bound to repeat it," Mr. Carlin, the history teacher, liked to quote to our class from George Santayana. I figured that the quotation could also apply to marriage. Unless I studied my parents' marriage, wasn't I bound to repeat their mistakes? I would observe their marriage impartially, looking for both positives and negatives and trying to see it from each parent's viewpoint.

My mother had wavy blond hair and what I thought of as an "objectively pretty" but somewhat square-jawed face, the kind I had seen described as "open."

She taught second grade at Friends Seminary. In the evenings, when she talked about her day in school—the deeds and misdeeds of her pupils—I felt as if I were following a radio serial, eagerly awaiting each new installment. Sometimes she consulted me on which books to use in class.

I told her that books that put faces on inanimate objects were condescending. "Kids want accuracy," I insisted, "not cars that smile and burp while being filled up with gasoline, or baby steam engines that cry when they're shifted onto a siding to let an express train pass by."

I fondly recalled a children's book I had had, showing the aircraft carrier Lexington sinking slowly, as the sailors sat on deck eating ice cream out of containers they had brought up from the ship's refrigerators, while awaiting their turns to abandon ship. Another favorite book had depicted early World War I German and Allied pilots in bi-planes, waving while they flew past each other on their way to observe troop positions. But one day, a German pilot dropped a brick on a French plane's wing, launching the age of aerial warfare.

My mother's father was German and her mother, Danish. After marrying in Germany, they emigrated to the United States and settled in Montclair, New Jersey, where my grandfather opened a camera store and the couple had three children. My mother was the youngest and the only girl.

Her father had hated life in Germany, she said. "*His* father was very strict. Whenever he spoke, the whole family had to keep their eyes lowered, even his wife. That was the German custom in those days. '*Augen neider!*' (Eyes down!), he would remind anyone who forgot."

My mother's father was the opposite: friendly and easy-going and liking to make fun of his German heritage. Only five foot, four, he would come into the house after work with a cigar in his mouth, bellowing, "Here comes the big German man!" He spoiled my mother, as did her two brothers, whom she adored. Only her mother was a little strict with her, "but in a nice Danish way."

While getting her Master's in education, my mother met

and fell in love with my father, then a lieutenant in the Army Veterinary Corps, and they married soon after she graduated.

"One thing I liked about your father right away," she said to me, "was that he got me to talk about myself. He seemed to care. I remember how delighted he looked when I told him that I loved taking care of children. I think he thought he could have children and I'd do the work of raising them."

"Mom," I asked, "don't you honestly think Dad would have been happier if you'd given birth to puppies, instead of Alice and me? Haven't you noticed how he likes to scratch our ears and rub our tummies, while we lie on our backs and put all four paws in the air? Or with you, how he pats you on the head and says, 'Good Karen!'"

"That's just his way of showing affection. As a vet, he's around animals all the time. It carries over to people unconsciously."

My mother was a practicing Quaker, and my father a nonreligious Jew. When I was twelve, the Jewish kids in my class were going to Hebrew school, to prepare for their Bar or Bas Mitzvahs.

"I'm glad I don't have to go," I announced to my parents. "I prefer having the free time."

"Frankly," said my father, "I would send you, whether you wanted to go or not. If only they taught the history of the Jews, without pushing the dogma. That's the problem. All of the rabbis indoctrinate, like the clergy in every other religion. But if you want to go we'll send you."

"No, I agree with you, Dad—I don't want to be indoctrinated." I sensed this was a more diplomatic response than repeating that I'd rather have the time free.

"I think you're making a big mistake," said my mother. "You should learn about your heritage."

"Well, I guess there's no harm in your trying it," my father agreed, "provided you keep your wits about you."

The following Sunday, I joined the Hebrew school class of

22

our neighborhood Reform Temple. The class that day was using clay and twigs to build miniature *sukkahs*—the covered shelters commemorating those used by the Jews while wandering in the wilderness. I set to work with clay and twigs, too. But instead of a *sukkah*, I modeled a submarine, using clay for the hull and conning tower and various size twigs for the "four-inch" cannon and the anti-aircraft guns. When I had nearly finished, the rabbi came over and asked what I was doing.

"I'm building a submarine," I said.

"We're not building submarines," said the Rabbi. "We're building sukkahs." He picked up my submarine, squashed it back into a lump of clay, and returned the twigs to the twig box. "You're preparing to become a man," said the rabbi. "*Verstehst?* Think of your parents. Would they rather you bring home a lousy submarine, or a nice *sukkah?*"

Even at twelve, I had thought the rabbi was loading the question. Why not a *lousy sukkah*, or a *nice* submarine?

"You were right," I said to my father when I got home: "The rabbi did try to indoctrinate me."

"I thought so. Tell me, what did he say?"

"He said that the Jewish god was stronger than the Christian god." Actually, another kid in the class had asked whether the Christian gods weren't "stronger in total," since they had three gods—the Trinity—while the Jews had only one. The rabbi had replied that the Jews' one god was as powerful as the Christian's three. But for that to be true, I calculated, the Jewish god had to be stronger than any of the Christian gods individually. Therefore, the rabbi had been trying to indoctrinate us.

That was my first and last day at Hebrew School, although I continued going to seders at friends' houses. Alice later went to Hebrew school at her own request and made her Bas Mitzvah.

I preferred accompanying my mother to Friends Meeting. A pamphlet in the meetinghouse lobby said that the name *Friends* came from the Quakers' name in 17th-century

23

England, "the friends of truth," and from Jesus' having called his disciples his friends.

I liked the element of surprise at Meeting—of never knowing who was going to speak next, or about what—and the Quaker custom that anyone could get up in Meeting and say anything, if moved to speak by the inner Spirit. An editor friend of my mother's compared going to Meeting to reading through a pile of unsolicited manuscripts—generally dull, but with occasional bright spots making it all worthwhile.

During one Meeting, nobody spoke for the first fifteen minutes. Then a thin, middle-aged man stood up to speak.

"I was riding my bicycle to work," he said, "and as I rode, I called out, 'Hello, hello,' to everyone I passed. Many people ignored me, but I got a lot of nice hellos back. I felt that we had exchanged something. I would call it—good feelings."

I admired the speaker. He was taking the risk of being thought weird, to spread around a little cheer.

After another ten minutes of silence, a second man got up to talk about snowflakes. "I was observing their crystalline structure one day last winter," he said, "when suddenly I realized how beautiful winter can be, even here in our city. Spirit moved me today to share that with you."

My mother took me out to lunch after Meeting. Over shrimp cocktail, which I seldom ordered when my father was along, lest he think me extravagant, we discussed the girls in my school.

"What matters most," said my mother, "isn't beauty, but character. That old saying is really true, you know—'beauty is only skin deep.'"

I tried taking the saying literally, picturing a girl with beautiful skin, but homely flesh and bones underneath. It was a tough image to form.

"I agree, with you, Mom," I said. "Character *is* more important. But why not begin looking for character among the attractive girls? Then, if they all lack character, I can turn to the plain ones with deep souls."

"I still say character is what counts," my mother insisted.

She also warned me against foreign girls, especially Mediterraneans. "They'll lead you around by the nose and you won't even know it, like the French and Italians did to poor President Wilson after World War One. He was too honest. The French know how to make words say one thing, but really mean the opposite. So, be on your guard, dear."

"I will, Mom," I said, although the only foreign girl I knew was a Canadian from Winnipeg, at school.

My mother went on to warn me about various improbable events. Don't get between a mother bear and its cubs. If you fall into quicksand, lie down flat and crawl out on all fours. In Penn Station, watch out for the electric baggage carts—the drivers never look where they're going.

I imagined myself falling into quicksand, being hit from behind by an electric baggage cart, or walking through a forest and inadvertently coming between a mother bear and its cubs. I wondered whether, if I kept circling around the base of a large tree, the mother bear would eventually get dizzy and stop chasing me.

> [The uninstructed man] does not
> know that there are numberless delicate dif-
> ferentiations and modifications of sexual
> pleasure, all lying strictly within the bounds
> of *normality*....
>
> *Ideal Marriage*, p. 8.

I felt bolder in questioning my mother than my father about sex. While my father responded with dissertations on how sex was "a perfectly normal human drive, if channeled correctly," and with lots of animal information I had no interest in—on milt and roe, plumage and mating dances—my mother tried to answer my questions as well as she could. She feared that refusing to answer could turn a child neurotic, a fear I exploited.

I liked to talk with my mother at night, before going to sleep. She would sit on the couch in my room, while I was already in bed with the table lamp off.

She said that, when she was growing up, girls were expected to remain virgins until marriage. "I think it made life easier. If I was dating a man and he broke up with me, I would have felt worse if I'd slept with him."

"Are you glad you stayed a virgin until you married Dad?" I asked.

"In those days, it wasn't an issue. Your father didn't have much experience either though he did have some definite ideas."

"What kind of ideas?" I felt my curiosity aroused.

"Nothing worth mentioning," said my mother. "Only that your father thinks that certain things are unnatural. *I* feel, if two people love each other, whatever they want to do is normal so long as it doesn't hurt anyone. But marriage would be dull if a couple agreed on everything."

"Mom, are you referring to oral sex? I'm not prying. I just want to avoid any misunderstanding."

"Dear, I think all this questioning is unhealthy."

"I honestly don't mean it that way. I promise. I'm only asking because I want to be a good husband myself someday. I want to learn how to make my own marriage as good as I can."

"Well, if you *must* know," said my mother, "the answer is yes."

"I'm sorry," I said. "I'm sorry Dad thinks oral sex is unnatural. He's wrong, you know?" I didn't want to reveal that my source was *Ideal Marriage.*

For a moment, I wished that incest wasn't forbidden and I could give my mother the pleasure my father was denying her. It wouldn't really be incest, I reasoned. I wouldn't be having intercourse with my mother, or competing with my father. I would just be adding an element he wasn't interested in.

"If you want to be a good husband," said my mother, "you should learn to be more thoughtful instead of asking so many questions. Women appreciate thoughtfulness in a man more than questions. You can begin by writing Grandma Schulman a thank-you note for the sweater she gave you three weeks ago.

I'm starting a new policy. For every question I answer, I'll assign you one task to help make you a better husband."

"Mom, that's unfair!" I felt tricked. "It will have a chilling effect on free speech."

"No, dear, it will have a warming effect on good deeds."

"Okay, okay," I said. "I'll write Grandma Schulman a thank-you note tomorrow. But tell me more one thing: If you had to do it all over again, would you still have married Dad?"

"Definitely! At times I could kill your father, but I love him very much."

I enlisted my sister's help in analyzing our parents' marriage. Alice made a natural ally. At 13½, having no romances of her own yet, she interested herself passionately in those of others, including our parents.

Alice and I would sit together late at night, in my room or hers, with a bottle of ginger ale between us. We poured "shots" from it into whiskey glasses while trading observations on our parents and comparing any differences we noticed in them on mornings after their door had been locked the previous night.

Alice was going through a time of trying out fancy words. "Talk Shakespeare," she would beg me, knowing I was reading *Hamlet* in school. Then we would carry on conversations filled with "methinks," "pray tell," and "good my liege."

A poem of hers titled "A Parrot Bit Me"—"A parrot bit me and my vision of life expanded"—had won second prize in a *World Telegram & Sun* poetry contest, in the fourteen-and-under category.

"I'm proud of you," I said to her.

Alice hugged me. "Andre, I feel so happy when you're proud of me."

But she could change in an instant, flaring up at my slightest criticism, which I'd thought merely a helpful suggestion.

Once when we were going out to dinner with our parents, I noticed a slight sweaty odor on Alice. I suggested to her that she might want to put on a little deodorant.

"Are you telling me I *stink?*" she asked.

"No, I'm not." I wanted to calm her. "It's only a little borderline, but why not play it safe and be sure?"

"Can't you say nice things instead of criticizing me?"

"Alice, it's not a criticism. I thought that you'd rather I mention it than have people turn away from you and you wonder why."

"I'm sorry you think I'm such a bad sister."

"No, you're a *fine* sister. I just want to help you to be even better." I knew I should have left off the last sentence. I tried to make up for it. "Alice, I'm sorry if I said something wrong. In the future, I'll leave it up to others to be the messenger."

"All right," she said. "I'll put on some deodorant. But I'll never speak to you again until you apologize to me sincerely."

"I apologize," I said. "I apologize sincerely."

"Andre, I'm suspicious of that apology. But I'll accept it, because I'm such a good person." It was something she often said about herself.

Some of our worst fights concerned presents. Alice liked to buy presents for others, but would get hurt if she felt that the receiver—I, in particular—didn't adequately reciprocate.

"It doesn't have to be a *big* present," she once said to me. "Although, mind you, I like big presents. I just want presents that show you thought about me—that you asked yourself, 'What would Alice think is special'?"

Shortly before her 13th birthday, Alice had taken four dollars out of my wallet to buy herself an *eau de toilette* as a "present" from me. In the evening she came into my room and confessed and gave me back the 31 cents change.

"I didn't *steal* the money," Alice insisted. "I *borrowed* it. I thought you'd want to get me a present I liked. But if I'm wrong, I'll give you the money back. I'll save it up from my allowance. That shows you what kind of person I am."

"You're a *thief*," I said. "That's the kind of person you are. If you wanted to *borrow* the money, why didn't you ask me?"

I was furious at Alice for stealing from my wallet. It made me feel unsafe for the future.

28

"The only reason I'm not reporting you to the police," I said to her, "is because you're my sister. That's why I'm giving you a chance to turn away from a life of crime before it's too late. I won't ask for the money back if you promise you'll never do it again."

Actually, Alice had saved me the trouble of shopping for her birthday. If I took the money back, I'd have to go shopping and buy her something else.

"Andre, I was wrong," she said, tearfully. "I promise."

"If you ever steal money from me again," I said, shaking a finger at her, "I'll never buy you another present in your *whole* life. And I'll find a way to hurt you back. Do you understand?"

"Yes." Alice was crying steadily. I gave her a Kleenex and followed her into her room.

"I want to tell you something for your own sake," I said. "Sit down." I sat on her desk chair, and she on her bed.

"Alice," I said, speaking extra calmly, like the menacing voice of the narrator in *Lights Out* on TV. "Alice, a life of crime often starts with just such a petty theft. You steal from your brother when he's not looking, or maybe from your mother's pocketbook. Then you branch out. You shoplift from a store. A set of jacks, a few Milky Way bars, a compact you wanted.

"Soon there's no turning back. You've become a career criminal. I know how it works. I've read about it."

What I had read was *The Amboy Dukes*, a novel about a Brooklyn teenager who joins a street gang and eventually dies in the chair for murder.

"You go on to grand larceny, next. It's just stealing over a hundred dollars worth. But one day, you get caught, and they send you to reform school till you're twenty-one.

"Do you know what it's like in reform school? Tough girls from Brooklyn and the Bronx will keep beating you up. And they'll do a lot worse things to you. Creepy things."

"Andre, stop!" Alice put her hands over her ears.

"Believe me, it's kinder of me to tell you before you get sent to reform school and come out a hardened criminal, ready to rob a bank. And while you're robbing it, maybe you kill someone—a teller who moves too slow, or presses the alarm. Then you're sent to the electric chair for murder.

"Alice, at breakfast tomorrow, look at the bacon cooking. Watch how it curls up, trying to get away from the heat. Listen to it sizzling and sputtering, and smell that pig flesh burning. That'll be *you*, Alice, frying in the electric chair."

"I'm telling!" She ran into our parents' room, sobbing to them that I was giving her nightmares.

But my father said to her, "Taking money from Andre's wallet was *stealing*. Frankly, I'm disappointed in you."

My mother said, "We don't *ever* take things from anyone without asking." For once, she didn't tell me to "make allowances for Alice" because she was younger than me.

"I'm sorry, I'm sorry," said Alice, still sobbing. "I promise I'll never do it again. But tell me I'm not going to die in the electric chair."

"Of course, you're not," said my mother. "Andre should apologize for scaring you like that."

"I apologize," I said to Alice. "And I apologize about the bacon sizzling and burning, like someone dying in the electric chair." I wanted Alice to keep that image of herself frying.

Now, half a year later, I tried to explain to her my viewpoint on presents. I said I considered it sufficient to buy her one present each for Christmas and her birthday. "You can't give someone lots of presents he hasn't asked for, to oblige him to give you a lot of presents back."

"You really hurt me," said Alice. "I'm not obliging you to do *anything*. I thought you'd want to give me presents because you care about your sister. I see I'm mistaken. I don't have a generous brother."

I wanted to end the fight, but didn't know how to do it, without accepting her unfair charges.

"I care a lot about you," I said. "But you can't measure love by the number of presents you get. That's materialistic."

"Now you're calling me *materialistic*? I don't think it's materialistic to want to get presents from my own brother, who I do so much for. You have to admit, Andre, I do a lot more for

30

you than you do for me."

"That's not true. When I give you *one* present, it's like your giving me *three*, because you like shopping more."

"Oh, so it's painful for you to shop for me."

I felt frustrated. Alice kept twisting my words and getting angrier at me. Was there no way out?

Maybe there *was*, I thought. I could use my fight with Alice as part of preparing for my own marriage. Supposing I found myself in a fight with my wife one day? How would I handle it differently?

I tried pretending that Alice was my wife, whom I adored and wanted to get back on loving terms with.

"Please forgive me," I said to her. "I got carried away and said things I don't mean at all. I *love* you. I don't want to hurt you. I want to make you happy. Can't we find a way back to each other—a compromise where we each give up a little and we both feel good about it?"

"I'd like that very much," said Alice. Her anger evaporated, replaced by tenderness and a hug.

My father grew up, an only child, in Stamford, Connecticut. His father had a local law practice in wills, land sales, and non-lucrative divorces—the rich hired New York lawyers. His mother taught English in high school and devoted her spare time to social causes—strengthening public education, supporting world federalism, and urging her pupils to become fighters against corporate and political abuses.

My father said that his mother had tried to discourage him from becoming a veterinarian. Why didn't he become a "real doctor" and help people, she demanded, or a lawyer and fight corruption? She told him that she had named him Ernest in the hope that he would take his "responsibilities as a citizen seriously."

Instead, he went to veterinary college at Cornell. He was disappointed to find it geared mainly to the needs of farmers. Two years of inoculating chickens, pushing everted uteruses

31

back into cows, and filing horses' teeth when they became too pointed convinced him that he didn't like all animals equally. He wanted a small-animal practice concentrated on dogs. After serving in the Army Veterinary Corps during World War II— inspecting meat and caring for guard dogs—he interned at the Animal Medical Center in New York, then opened his own practice. Almost immediately he began yearning for the day when he could afford to eliminate cats from it.

"It's funny," he said to me, "when I'm treating a dog, I just want to help the poor beastie. But with cats, I admit to a little materialism. I think about what I'll do with the money I'm earning. It takes my mind off the unpleasantness of handling them."

Early one Sunday morning, my father and I were sitting alone in the living room, doing the crossword puzzle. While he filled in most of the words, I felt proud when I could help with an occasional sports definition, such as "The Super Swedish Angel," for "Wrestler known to rub soap in his opponents' eyes."

"One of the saddest experiences of my life occurred three years ago," said my father. "As I was returning to my office after lunch one day, I noticed two boys—about eleven or twelve—walking in front of me. I overheard one of them say to the other, 'If you love your dog, don't take him to Doctor Schulman.'

"I recognized the boy who said it. His Scotty had died on my operating table while I was trying to relieve an intestinal blockage. Intellectually, I know there was nothing I could have done to save that dog. He was thirteen, the poor old thing. 'If you love your dog, don't take him to Doctor Schulman.' It still bothers me when I think about it."

I touched my father's elbow, wanting to comfort him. The boy's comment was unfair. I recalled my father's kindness toward animals—how tenderly he would cradle a young puppy in his arms to keep it warm while examining it; how gently he would remove glass from a cat's paw, or porcupine quills from a dog's face.

32

At other times, though, he criticized me in the guise of talking to one of his patients.

"I know you feel betrayed, Alphonse," he said to a beagle that was looking even sadder than usual, after receiving a distemper shot. "But think how *I* feel, having a son who walks into my office with his shirttails hanging out. You and I know, Alphonse, that a bedraggled coat is usually a sign of disease." Then addressing a cat that was licking itself, my father said, "Minette, *you* understand the importance of being clean. Andre could learn a lot from the animals, if he'd only pay attention."

I wondered if cats were really so clean. Wasn't their licking themselves all the time deceptive, giving them a spotless exterior at the price of dirty insides?

The problem, I thought, was that my father was the one who determined what I should learn from the animals. Beavers building, cats washing, squirrels hiding nuts—all were fitted to whatever lesson he was pushing at the time. He even used his animal knowledge to ruin movies for Alice and me when we were younger. If a beautiful woman in a safari film screamed inside her tent while a leopard was clawing at the outside, my father would lean over to us and say, "I hope you know that the scenes were shot at different times? The woman wasn't really inside the tent while the leopard was trying to get in."

As I grew older, I came to anticipate him. "Dad, please let me enjoy the elephants attacking the village. Tell me the fake parts after the movie's over."

My father came into my room one evening after dinner and sat down on the couch next to me.

"Can we talk a little?" he asked.

"Sure," I said, trying to sound open, while feeling wary. I reluctantly put down *The Cruel Sea*.

"I want you to know that Mom and I are proud of you, of how well you're doing in school." My father squeezed my right shoulder and scratched the backs of my ears, and I felt myself relaxing. "Tell me, though," he said, "is there anything bothering you, anything at all? I'd like to be of help to you, if you'll permit me."

"Thanks. But there's nothing I can think of." I wondered if I should invent something minor, before he hit on anything important.

"Well, if you *do* have any problems," he repeated, "I hope you'll confide in me. You know, I really care about you, fellow." He squeezed my shoulder again.

"I care about you, too, Dad." I felt close to him.

"I'm glad we talked," he said. He stood up to go. On his way out, he paused at the doorway. "By the by," he said, "I forget. Have we ever talked about masturbation?"

"Masturbation?" I tried to sound casual while feeling panic rush in. Had I been discovered? Had my father seen me through the bathroom keyhole, in spite of my always turning the key to vertical?

"My memory is that we haven't talked about it," he said. "Please correct me if I'm wrong." He returned to the couch and sat down again.

"Masturbation is a funny business," he said, and leaned back and stretched. "All those theories about its leading to disease or blindness are sheer nonsense. They're spread by ignorant, neurotic people, who should know better. Like one of my clients. This woman told me that she gets upset whenever her dachshund licks his penis. As soon as he starts, she pushes cold compresses on him."

I joined my father in laughing at the woman's foolishness.

"What *is* true, however," he said, "is that *excessive* masturbation may have injurious psychological consequences. It can interfere with a young man's ability to develop healthy relations with a member of the opposite sex. And that can cause difficulties later on when it comes to marriage. But mind you, I'm not asking any questions."

"Thanks for telling me, Dad. I appreciate it." I ignored his implied question.

I admired my father's reasonableness. Unlike many parents, he didn't condemn masturbation. He just pointed out that only in excess was it harmful.

But how much was *excessive*? I wanted to get the benefits of masturbating without its hurting me psychologically. I had viewed it as medicinal—a measure to prevent wet dreams, with their telltale odors and stains—as well as a gauge of my feelings for a particular girl. I would masturbate while imagining I was making love with her. After reaching orgasm, I would re-examine my feelings for the girl. If she no longer appealed to me, I concluded that I'd felt only lust for her. If she still attracted me, it could be love.

I usually masturbated in the bathroom, while flipping through the pictures in the *New York Times Magazine* or my mother's issues of *Vogue*. One underwear ad, captioned, "I dreamed I went to blazes in my Maidenform Bra," showed a woman in short shorts and a white bra, riding on the running board of a fire engine at night. She was holding on with one hand while her other arm was outstretched, wearing what looked like a Wonder Woman bracelet. I imagined her returning to me afterwards, slipping off her bra and shorts, and telling me that *I* was the "blaze" she had been thinking about while fighting the fire.

I sometimes helped my father out after school, to earn money and try to put him in a good mood for questioning. I cleaned out the cages of the animals being kept overnight for observation, prepared fecal smears for microscopic analysis, and helped the owners hold their pets steady on the table while my father examined them and gave them injections. I imagined developing a method of curving a puppy's bones, while they were still young enough to be malleable, and molding them to the dimensions of the owner's yard. Then whenever the dog was let out, it would necessarily run in an arc and never stray off the property, even without a fence. ("Don't push on your sister's head," my mother had once said to me when Alice was four. "Her bones are still soft—you could deform her skull." Only much later did I find out that an infant's bones had already

35

hardened by age two.)

One day, a tall man in the uniform of an Air Force colonel strode into my father's office, leading an Alaskan malamute that was suffering from gallstones. Part of the malamute's left side was shaved bare, and on it were tattooed four cat heads, just as the number of enemy aircraft shot down were painted on the fuselage of warplanes.

The malamute's appearance enraged a woman whose two cats were awaiting anti-respiratory-infection shots. "How can you treat that monster?" she asked my father after the malamute and its owner had left.

"I appreciate your feelings," said my father. "But as a veterinarian, I'm obliged to heal *every* animal, whatever I may think of it personally, or of its owner."

I looked down to avoid smiling. I shared my father's aversion to cats. While a dog could be muzzled on the examining table, if a cat got even one paw free I was in trouble.

After seeing his last patient, my father invited me to a soda fountain on our way home. We sat at the counter, since at a table, the waitress would have brought only a glassful each of the frosteds we ordered—my father, strawberry, and I, coffee—not the entire metal container, holding a glass and three-quarters worth. I drank my frosted right from the glass, without using a straw. A soda jerk had once told me that a straw cut down on the pleasure: "The drink misses half of your taste buds, and you get no feeling of it around your lips."

"Don't tell your mother about the frosted," said my father. "She'll accuse me of spoiling your appetite."

"I won't say a word," I promised, enjoying the feeling of being in a conspiracy with my father.

"Speaking of Mom," I said, sensing my opportunity, "if you had it to do over again, would you still have married her? I mean, if you feel free to tell me."

"You pose a difficult question," said my father. "Permit me to parse it out aloud. When your mother and I married, I had had hardly any sex experiences—a mistake, incidentally, that I hope you won't repeat." He sighed. "Yes, I've sometimes want-

36

ed to make a fresh start. But I couldn't have lived with myself if I'd broken up the family. To answer your question, if I had it to do over again, I would probably have waited to get married until I'd had more experiences."

"And once you'd *had* those experiences, would you still have married Mom, eventually?"

"On balance, I would say, yes. Whatever her faults, your mother's an awfully nice person, as I'm sure you'll agree. But there *are* certain problems. I just can't get interested in what little Tommy did in school every day. Or how little Rachel knew what 'baggage car' meant without having to look it up. There are also certain other things that I shouldn't go into, that belong just between Mom and me."

"I understand," I said, wondering what those "other things" were. "Is there anything I can do to help?" I stopped myself from bringing up oral sex, from suggesting that Mom would like it if he went down on her.

"No, there's nothing for you to do," said my father. "Except stop being so curious."

I silently vowed that I'd never feel about my own wife merely that, "on balance," I would marry her again.

Some days later, while rummaging through my mother's closet, I found an old letter to her from my father. "Karen dearest," it read:

> It's only a week before our wed-
> ding, and I still can't believe that I'm so
> fortunate: that you truly want to marry me!
> I'm counting the days and hours.
>
> My darling mouse, I promise
> always to try to be worthy of you,
>   Your *ecstatic* Ernest.

What had happened since then, I wondered, to turn "Your *ecstatic* Ernest" into "On balance, I would do it again"?

I thought about Van der Velde's dedication to his wife in

Ideal Marriage: "Because every day I love you more. Today more than yesterday and much less than tomorrow."

I would make it my life's work to travel Van der Velde's road, rather than my father's.

Chapter Three

JESSICA

> We hardly dare nowadays, to admit that
> two human beings loved one another because
> they looked at one another. Yet—love dawns
> thus, and only thus. The rest—comes after-
> wards. Nothing is more true, more real, than
> the primeval magnetic disturbances that two
> souls may communicate to one another,
> through the tiny spark of a moment's glance.
>
> *Ideal Marriage*, page 43

I MET JESSICA Dane on the first Saturday in October, during an afternoon boat trip around Manhattan. I had spent the morning in the Public Library on 42nd Street, trying to write a paper on Louis XVI for my history class. But after two hours, I had managed only to copy down an opening quotation, reading, "From the tip of his toes to the top of his head, Louis XVI formed a perfect butterball," and then to add three pages of random facts, culled from three encyclopedias. I knew I had done better in my fifth-grade book report on *All Conference Tackle*.

But what did it matter? I thought. The Russians had launched Sputnik the day before. At any time, they might drop a bomb on us from it as Sputnik passed overhead beyond the range of our defenses. I felt panic rising in me. I didn't want to spend what could be my last day on earth, sitting in the library, writing about Louis XVI and maybe winding up burned to a crisp in my chair. I needed at least one more look at the outside world.

I hurried down the stairs of the library and headed west on 42nd Street. As I walked along, I began to feel better. Others out on the street seemed unconcerned. The day was cloudy, but pleasant. The temperature on an electric sign showed 63. While I still thought of Sputnik circling high above the clouds, it struck me that the Russians might target Washington first, to destroy our Government. Or maybe Hollywood, to prevent the movie industry from making any more anti-Soviet films. Or someplace like Kansas City or Des Moines, as a warning to us of what the Russians could do if we didn't accept their terms on "normalizing" Berlin. The risk of New York's being bombed without warning now seemed reduced, from a near certainty, to less than one-third.

I stopped in at Grant's for lunch—a small, but juicy hamburger for 17 cents, a cup of French fries (which I extended with catsup) and a small chocolate soda for 5 cents each.

Then I continued west on 42nd Street. As I walked along, regretting the days' growing shorter and checking out the marquees of double-feature porno theaters, I came upon a Circle Line hawker, announcing that the next trip around Manhattan would leave in 20 minutes. I decided on an impulse to take it.

For the first hour and a half, I stood out on deck, identifying ships in dock and familiar buildings we passed. I reflected that maybe I should see a porno film before dying, before Khrushchev finally carried out his threat to "bury" us. Then when the air turned cool around four, as we passed from the Harlem River into the broader, windier Hudson, I went indoors to the cafeteria and ordered a hot chocolate. I sat down with it at one of the long tables, across from a girl with light brown hair, a radiant smile, and sparkling-clean ears.

"I see you like hot chocolate, too," I said, noticing she had a cup of it in front of her.

"I do," she said. "I love marshmallows in hot chocolate, even though they bump your nose." She wrinkled her nose and smiled, showing blue eyes and teeth so white that I closed my mouth to hide my own fillings.

"Would you like my marshmallow?" I asked her.

"No, I can't deprive you—"

"Please, I would like you to have it. They dropped it into my cup without asking me." If it had been whipped cream, I might not have offered her any, I thought. I liked the way whipped cream filtered the heat of the hot chocolate and gave me both tastes—chocolate and whipped cream—simultaneously. With a marshmallow, though, I could afford to be generous.

"Well, thank you," she said.

I spooned my marshmallow into her cup, then said, "Incidentally, I'm Andre Schulman." I felt relieved that I'd had fried, rather than raw onions on my hamburger at lunch.

"Jessica Dane," she said, and introduced the man and woman on her left and right as her parents.

Luckily, I hadn't known that they were her parents, I thought. I might have felt too shy to introduce myself to her.

"I'm pleased to meet you," said her father, reaching out to shake hands with me.

Her mother said she was glad to meet a native New Yorker. They lived in Concord, Massachusetts, where Jessica was a junior in high school. They were visiting New York for the weekend.

I hung out with them for the rest of the trip. I pointed out New York landmarks a moment before the loudspeaker did, and I glanced at Jessica as much as possible without making it obvious.

"Would you join us for dinner?" her father asked me, before we landed. "We were planning to go to Manny Wolf's Steak House."

"Unless, as a New Yorker, you have another suggestion?" said her mother.

"No, Manny Wolf's is a great choice." I felt delighted at their invitation. "Thank you very much. But I don't want to interfere with your plans."

"You're not," said Jessica's mother. Would you like to call your parents first and make sure it's okay? You can phone from our hotel. We're staying at the Plaza. We have to go back there anyway to change."

"I *would* like to call them," I said, not mentioning that I'd forgotten about it.

I had also forgotten that the restaurant required a jacket and tie, but the maitre d' lent me a brown herringbone jacket and a solid-blue tie.

I ordered the chopped steak, having seen it was the cheapest meat dish on the menu. Jessica ordered lamb chops, her father a sirloin steak, and her mother the "junior sirloin." I would have liked to have a sirloin, too, but I thought it impolite to order an expensive dish when invited out, unless I was urged to do so.

Looking at Jessica, I felt scared and elated. She was beautiful! She had changed into a cream-colored blouse with translucent sleeves and neckline area, and she was wearing a gold butterfly pin with little blue stones on it. Her skin was so smooth that I had to restrain my hand from caressing her. I half-wished she had a mildly disfiguring scar, so other boys would overlook her, while her smile alone would have been enough to attract me. I read into it sweetness, intelligence, and a hint of irreverence.

Her father was a banker, the American director and vice-president of a Dutch bank. Listening to him talk, I thought I might become a banker, too. I had never realized before that banking could be so interesting, at least Dutch banking. I pictured myself as a minor loan officer in his bank, bicycling through the Dutch countryside, scouting for small projects for the bank to finance—dairy farms, herring boats, gin distilleries—and stopping beside canals for lunches of bread, cheese, and chocolate.

Partway through dinner, Jessica's mother, whom I had been calling 'Mrs. Dane,' said to me, "I'm Maude and he's Oliver," and I felt a rush of warmth toward both of them.

Unfortunately, I realized, I was often more popular with parents than with their daughters. I wished it were reversed—that mothers, instead of holding me up as a model, would warn their daughters against me, fearing for their virginity, but that their daughters would be fatally drawn to me, sneaking out to meet me without their parents' knowledge.

After dinner, we all walked along Fifth Avenue together. I showed them Rockefeller Center, Tiffany's, and the Squibb Building where my dentist's office was. I also pointed out the RCA Building and said it was the third-tallest building in New York.

"I didn't know *that*," said Jessica's mother, gazing at me, as if she had just made an important confession and wanted to make sure I realized it. "You see how lucky we are to have met you, Andre?"

I felt a little uneasy under her gaze, and her praise of me seemed excessive, unearned by anything I had done.

Jessica announced that she hoped to visit the Museum of Modern Art.

"Would you like to go tomorrow?" I asked her. "We could go together, if you've got the time?" I looked down, to hide my eagerness.

Jessica asked her parents, who agreed, provided she got back to the hotel by four. They had been invited for an early dinner by friends in Hoboken.

"Supposing I pick you up at eleven?" I said, trying to sound casual.

Jessica clapped her hands and bounced up and down. "I'm so excited," she said. "I've never seen the Museum of Modern Art. But if you don't like museums, tell me. Be honest. I wouldn't want you to go just for me."

"No, I do like them. I *do*." I imagined saying, "I do," at my wedding to Jessica.

Actually, I remembered having felt bored at the Museum of Modern Art. I had visited it a month earlier, determined, as a junior in high school, to try to understand and appreciate modern art. But even when, with Cubism, I could make out a fragmented face, superimposed on a guitar neck and chair back, the paintings still left me cold. Nor, after the novelty wore off, had I gone for Mondrian's geometric grids; Picasso's distorted people and animals; or various artists' circles and bulls-eyes, triangles and rectangles, or canvasses filled with a single solid color. I had to admit, a bit ashamed of myself, that I preferred Lucas Cranach's dogs lapping from a bowl.

After a while, my attention turned from looking at the paintings to thinking about Georgio de Chirico.

A museum tour guide had said that, unlike with most artists, de Chirico's later paintings sold for less than his earlier works, and that, therefore, he had later tried to return to his former style of painting and had "forged" earlier dates on the later paintings.

At first I felt sorry for de Chirico, for having lost a talent he had once had. Then I grew indignant on his behalf. "It's his own business when he finishes a painting!" I argued silently, as if defending him. Anyway, why did he have to put on the date on which he had *finished* the painting? What about the date he started it, or first had the idea for it?

Only later did I realize that I'd been so absorbed with de Chirico's cause that I'd hardly noticed much of the art I was walking past. Now I wished I had paid more attention, so I could have discussed it intelligently with Jessica the next day.

"My parents think you have fine manners," Jessica said to me, when I picked her up at her hotel next morning. "My mother says it's a sign of good character. Pah! Some of the boys I know with the best manners are real stinkers underneath. Or they're drips."

"I know what you mean," I said, thinking I'd rather be considered a stinker than a drip.

In the museum Jessica and I compared which animals the various Miro paintings reminded us of. Jessica saw dogs, ponies, and spiders; I saw chickens, sheep, and rodents—the kind that in Disney movies emerged from their burrows after the flood waters had receded, while the narrator intoned, "And life returns once more to the valley."

I liked going through the museum with Jessica. Expecting her to be earnest and knowledgeable, I found her playful instead.

"I think art's boring if you take it too seriously," she said. "Like, Arshile Gorky's paintings remind me of clumpier Miros."

"I agree," I said, thinking I could see what she meant. "To me, Motherwell's paintings look like kabobs of shashlik."

We both turned serious in front of Munch's "The Silent Scream."

"I feel incredibly lucky," said Jessica, "to be standing in front of this painting, instead of feeling whatever was making the man scream."

"I feel incredibly lucky, too," I said, thinking *lucky to be with Jessica*. She was not only beautiful and intelligent, but sensitive as well.

"I love you," I said to her, silently. And after saying it, I felt that everything had changed for me. I would have liked to spend the rest of our museum visit just looking at Jessica, instead of the art. Or, at most, taking in the art indirectly, by observing Jessica looking at it. Then she would become part of each painting for me. I noticed a few tendrils of her hair hanging down from the rest. If only I knew her well enough to reach out and brush them back up, caressing her cheek as I did so.

Every few minutes, I checked my watch, thinking about lunch. Finally, at 1:55, I said, "Shall we get a bite to eat? The cafeteria should be emptying out by now."

Having made it through a morning of art, I felt that with food I would be on more familiar ground.

The museum cafeteria offered a choice of sandwiches, identifiable less by taste than by variously-colored strips of paper on each plate. Jessica had a ham sandwich with bright yellow mustard; I had a "cold platter" of underdone chicken, bloody near the drumstick bone and with nubby skin. For dessert we both took lemon pie, with meringues so rubbery they slid off of the filling in one piece.

"Jessica," I said to her before getting up from the table, "could I possibly ask you for your address? I would like to keep in touch, if it's all right with you?" I wanted to let her know now that I was interested in her, not keep her waiting until the last minute, when it could be embarrassing if her parents were there.

"I would love to keep in touch," she said. "It's rare that I meet a boy who likes museums, too.

I felt like a fraud. I recalled the time I had praised a friend's mother's apple brown betty, which I'd barely been able to get down my throat, only to have it served again the next time I was there for dinner.

Jessica wrote my address in a notebook she carried in her purse. Having no notebook, I wrote her address on the two thin strips of colored paper identifying our museum meals, and as a back-up, I re-wrote it lightly on my school bus pass.

We left the museum soon after lunch, to get Jessica back to her hotel by four. Feeling expansive now that we were leaving, I suggested we look into one more gallery on our way out. It was bare, except for a series of wire coat hangers bent into various shapes and mounted on all four walls. The accompanying description said that the artist was "exploring reality on three levels: the texture and shape of the hangers themselves; their varying relationships to the walls; and the interplay of the hangers and the walls with the shadows cast by the hangers." I felt glad that it was our final gallery, rather than the beginning of our museum visit.

I took Jessica's hand when we turned onto Fifth Avenue and headed toward her hotel. As we walked, I thought about kissing her. But I wondered whether our merely having gone to a museum during the daytime counted as a real date. Even if it did, it was only a first date. She might resent my trying to kiss her so soon.

Yet, Jessica would be leaving tomorrow morning. I wouldn't get another chance to kiss her, and if I didn't even try, she might consider me one of the "drips" she had been talking about, which would be worse than trying too soon.

Also, I had a dental appointment the next Friday to have a cavity filled—a lower-jaw cavity. If I kissed Jessica now, then I could relive the kiss while Doctor Shimkin was drilling, and it would lessen the pain.

That decided it! I told myself. I would try to kiss her. Yet, as we kept walking, my anxiety increased. Feeling my hand growing sweaty, I let go of Jessica's. I realized that I was hardly noticing any of the buildings we passed—I had made myself point out the Fifth Avenue Presbyterian Church, lest Jessica think I was hurrying her by everything.

Now we were already at 58th Street. In half a block we would reach her hotel.

"How long is your train ride home tomorrow?" I asked, thinking I should say something, not just suddenly kiss her.

"Five hours," she said.

"Oh, I'm sorry, that's a long ride. But I'm glad you came." I felt proud of thinking of my last phrase.

"I'm *very* glad I came," said Jessica. "Anyway, I like trains and I can study on them."

"I love trains," I said. I thought that, as long as I kept talking, I might keep away my nervousness about kissing her.

We walked slowly down the 14th floor corridor to her hotel room, letting another couple go on ahead. Then a maid approached from the other direction. When the corridor was clear, I kissed Jessica quickly, before someone else came along.

I was so happy at kissing Jessica, it took me a moment to realize she was kissing me back. Her lips felt soft, yet alive. Her arms around my neck were wonderfully cool.

At first, I kissed her with my eyes closed. Then I opened them and saw her looking at me.

My anxiety evaporated. I caressed her face and the back of her neck, as I'd seen couples do in movies. Now I felt master of the logistics: one hand around Jessica's shoulder, holding her to me as I kissed her; my other hand making little crescents on her cheek with my fingertips. I would have liked to kiss her eyelids, too, but I feared being a little off and bumping her eye.

"I'd better go in now," she said, finally. "My parents'll be wondering. Andre, thank you for taking me to the museum. I'm so happy we went. And thanks for lunch."

"You're welcome," I said. "But I apologize that you had to eat bland food and rubbery lemon pie."

47

"No, it was part of my New York visit."

"Good night," I said. I kissed her once more, and this time while kissing her, I pictured the dentist drilling in my mouth. It seemed benign now. I wouldn't mind going to the dentist, if each time I could kiss Jessica first.

I stepped back to let her open the door, feeling responsible to her parents for Jessica's being on time. I imagined myself becoming their son-in-law.

After Jessica went in, I lingered awhile outside her door, pressing two fingers to my lips, as if still kissing her.

In the bus going home I sat on the left side, since the right was more crowded. I figured that, by balancing the weight distribution, I would lower the chance of the bus's flipping over if it stopped short or swerved. Even if that risk was tiny, why run it unnecessarily, especially now that I'd met Jessica? She gave me all the more reason to maximize my odds of staying alive. While I couldn't do anything about the main danger—dying from a nuclear bomb—sitting on the less-crowded side of the bus made me feel I wasn't completely helpless.

I walked home from school the next day through Central Park, enjoying the foliage without my father along. I lifted my face to the brightly-colored leaves—yellow and orange and red—and I rejoiced in my happiness at having kissed Jessica. I even looked up some of the tree names on plaques—Ginko, London plain, White Ash. I wanted to tell Jessica about them.

At the sailboat pond near 74th Street, I watched kids and old men sailing their model boats. I remembered years earlier, worrying about my own sailboat's getting becalmed or slammed against the pond's edge by a shifting gust of wind. The men used canes with soft tips to stop their boats in time and turn them around. The kids relied on their own hands, agility, and scampering power. Those kids with larger boats sometimes aimed them at smaller boats, hoping to ram and capsize them.

I looked at the statue of Alice in Wonderland, at the north end of the pond. She had such a sweet, pretty face, I thought. I smiled at her, imagining she was Jessica, my own Alice. "I love you," I said to her, quietly. Then I felt sorry for the nearby stat-

ue of Hans Christian Anderson, who had only the Ugly
Duckling for company.

A letter arrived from Jessica four days later, on Thursday:

> Dear Andre,
>   I have never had as much fun at a muse-
> um as with you. My old boyfriend, Michael,
> refused to go to museums. Ever. He even
> objected when I went alone. He thought I was
> criticizing him.
>   After meeting you, I know I could never
> go back to Michael. So I'm glad I met you for
> two reasons: 1. Because you're fun. (Or
> should I say, you're fun, so far?) 2. Because
> meeting you confirms that I was right to break
> up with Michael.

Her letter went on to invite me to visit her over
Thanksgiving, from Wednesday to Saturday. "My parents and I
thought you might enjoy a New England family Thanksgiving."

I read the letter three times in a row and again before going
to sleep. I felt blissful at her invitation—it meant she wanted to
see me again—and at having aced out her old boyfriend. Yet, I
was a little disappointed that Jessica had signed her letter,
"Can't wait to hear from you," instead of, "Love." If I were
writing to someone I had already kissed, I thought, I would sign
my letter, "Love," especially if that was how I felt.

But maybe she was waiting for me to sign, "Love," first. I
would write to her tomorrow and do so.

After dinner, I did homework until Alice and my parents
had gone into their rooms and closed the doors. Then I took
down *Ideal Marriage*. I would read it more urgently now. My
time-scale had changed. Marriage was no longer a vague
thought for the future, with no one in mind—that was, assum-
ing that Jessica would want to marry me, too. I could even

imagine us marrying after graduation from high school.

Waiting until after college seemed such a waste—four additional years, during which we could have been living together, going to classes during the day and reuniting each evening for dinner. Even on nights of studying late, we would take measured breaks—maybe, five minutes an hour—to hold hands and kiss, a miniature bliss in itself. Eventually, we would put away our books. Jessica would change into a nightgown and I into pajamas, and we would reach out to each other.

I started reading *Ideal Marriage* from the beginning again. I liked the beginning, because it promised so much.

"I show you here the way to Ideal Marriage," Chapter One opened.

> You know the honeymoon of rapture. It is all too short, and soon you decline into that morass of disillusion and depression, which is all you know of marriage.

> But the bridal honeymoon should blossom into the perfect flower of ideal marriage.

What a wonderful idea, I thought: to live my entire marriage as a honeymoon of rapture, blossoming into an ideal marriage. I read on:

> The four cornerstones of the temple of love and happiness in marriage are:—
> (1) A right choice of marriage partner.

Well, I had already made that "right choice." And if Jessica wouldn't marry me, I told myself, bravely, at least reading *Ideal Marriage* would leave me that far ahead for someone else.

I closed the book and put the last movement of Beethoven's Ninth Symphony onto my phonograph. He was my favorite composer, although his final bars often reminded me of the rhythm of a dog heaving up grass it had swallowed.

Tonight, I just wanted to fall asleep listening to Beethoven's Ninth. I looked up at the four glowing constellations—Orion, the Big Dipper, the Little Dog, and Cassiopeia—which I had cut out of pieces of blue fluorescent paper and pasted up on my ceiling. They shone in the dark for an hour after I turned out the lights. I pictured my honeymoon with Jessica "blossoming into the perfect flower of ideal marriage." Tomorrow, I would go on learning how to make that ideal a reality.

Chapter Four

DOCTOR SHIMKIN

> Carious teeth ... can be the *coup-de-grace* of love.
>
> *Ideal Marriage*, p. 27.

IN DOCTOR SHIMKIN'S waiting room, I picked up a children's book titled *Robert Visits The Dentist*. Nine-year-old Robert receives an injection of Novocain and smilingly tells the dentist, "It didn't hurt. I felt only a little pinch."

The book should be stamped "Deceptive!" I thought. It was unfair to little children, who might believe it and then feel betrayed.

I closed my eyes for about thirty seconds. I had dreamt one night that three gold inlays had fallen out in my mouth while I was waiting for the dentist. On awakening, I was elated to discover that I had only been dreaming. Since then, I've always closed my eyes in the waiting room, hoping on re-opening them to find myself back in my own bedroom.

I feared the dentist less today than on previous visits. I wanted to test whether reliving my kiss with Jessica would make the drilling less painful. Even if it didn't work, I thought—even if the drilling hurt as much as before—my undergoing it expressed my love for Jessica. I was preventing what *Ideal Marriage* called the odor of "carious teeth." In a way it seemed romantic, accepting present pain for the sake of our future love.

Doctor Shimkin was a Czech émigré with a kind manner, thick, unruly white hair, and a tendency to breathe heavily while working. He practiced in the days before the high-speed drill, when preparing to fill even a small cavity meant several changes of burs.

Now he started in drilling with a large, noisy bur, which his hygienist called "the rock." It screamed and sent vibrations throughout my head, keeping me tense and my jaw opened wide, lest the "rock" graze my cheek and gouge out a piece of it. Then Shimkin switched to progressively finer and quieter burs. Yet, the quieter the bur, the more it hurt.

At first, I tried to blot out the pain by reliving my kiss with Jessica. It didn't work. The drilling overrode my memories of kissing her, as well as any comfort from imagining I was enduring the pain for her sake. The limits of love were reached at dentistry.

During breaks for rinsing, I asked questions, hoping to prolong the respite.

"Doctor Shimkin, when did the people in Czechoslovakia first realize that the Nazis would march in?"

"Not soon enough," he said. "Please, open!" And the drilling continued.

From time to time, Shimkin squirted in air under pressure to dry out the cavity. The more the air hurt, I figured, the more the drilling to come also would hurt.

A steady rain fell outside. The rain, the stark dental lamp shining on my face, and Doctor Shimkin's hairy fingers in my mouth, forcing it wide open, all contributed to my feeling of being cut off from the world, in a gloomy, unsettling environment. The only window in the room faced another office building a few feet away, which looked drab even on sunny days. Looking at its windows, hoping for a little voyeurism, I saw only occasional cleaning ladies wringing out mops or other dental patients seemingly jerking in pain.

Doctor Shimkin paused in his drilling and shook his head.

"*Ja!*" he sighed. "What to do next? I have two choices: amalgam or gold. Which to choose?"

"How about amalgam?" I said, surprising myself at speaking out, since I realized that Doctor Shimkin wasn't asking my opinion. But I knew that gold would require more drilling than amalgam and at least one extra session to shape the inlay— repeatedly pushing it into and prying it out of my mouth and drilling on the inlay until it fit, then cementing it in.

"You don't want gold," said Doctor Shimkin. "I don't want to make gold. It's more work for me, and it costs more for you. Gold is a precious metal. Hmm. But amalgam is too risky. I call Miss Powderpuff to have a look." (She was Doctor Shimkin's hygienist and her name was Potapov, but he pronounced it *Powderpuff*.)

Doctor Shimkin held a mirror next to my decayed tooth and poked it with a scaler while Miss Potapov looked on.

"I see," she said. "Not enough enamel support."

"*Ja*, now I think we could use an injection," said Shimkin.

I gripped both the arm of the chair and Miss Potapov's hand while the long needle for a lower-jaw injection went in deeper and deeper. Then I enjoyed a brief pause for the Novocain to take effect—an interval that seldom seemed long enough.

"I'm just curious, Doctor Shimkin," I said, when he was about to start in drilling soon after the injection. "How long does it take for Novocain to deaden the tooth completely? I've noticed that sometimes you wait a little longer." Surely, even the time taken up by my asking the question would help the Novocain to work.

"Ooch," said Doctor Shimkin, "it only takes maybe couple of minutes. We try. If tooth isn't dead yet, we wait a little more. Okay? I am very surprised if you are feeling anything."

Doctor Shimkin proved right—the drilling didn't hurt. But now I worried about *not* feeling any pain. hat if the drill cut into my cheek or tongue without my realizing it, because the Novocain had deadened half of my mouth? I tried to keep my tongue far away from the drill, and I rinsed my mouth often to check for excessive bleeding. Miss Potapov had once confided that the reason that dentists used pink mouthwash was to mask any bleeding. So when Shimkin wasn't looking, I poured out the mouthwash and filled the cup with clear water instead.

After Shimkin finally put in a temporary filling and discharged me for the day, my mother took me to Hick's for a hot fudge sundae. I tried to keep the ice cream and hot fudge on the side of my mouth not numbed by the Novocain. But some of the ice cream and sauce slipped over, making me lose its taste and sensations. At dinner that evening, I ate the tomato soup in tiny spoonfuls, lest it burn me without my realizing it.

Going to the dentist had made me more mature about love, I told myself. Now I realized that love couldn't do everything—that it couldn't mask the pain of drilling. Therefore, I would love Jessica all the better for my love's being grounded in reality.

When I was thirteen and a half, I'd had so many cavities that Doctor Shimkin referred me to a children's dentist, Doctor Mandelbaum. He looked about 50 years old, wore an orange smock, and covered his office walls with paintings done by his patients. I wondered whether he hung the paintings because he had no diplomas.

"Yes, we have a lot of cavities," Dr. Mandelbaum said, smiling. (He wouldn't smile if they were his own cavities, I thought.) "But I promise that you'll like me."

I didn't like him.

"I'll tell you a secret," he said, leaning toward me and almost whispering. "I believe in being honest with my patients. You want me to be honest with you, Andre, don't you?"

"Yes," I said, weakly, feeling coerced.

"We have sixteen cavities to fill," said Doctor Mandelbaum. "Our word for cavities is *caries*." He wrote it in chalk on a portable blackboard on wheels. "I bet most of your classmates don't know the word. Now you know something they don't." He smiled again. He seemed to be always smiling.

"Before we begin," he asked, "do you have any questions? They don't have to be about dentistry. Sometimes, it helps to talk with a stranger about problems at home or at school."

"Will you give me Novocain?" I asked.

"If necessary," he said. "I know that some dentists always

give their patients Novocain. But I like to treat each tooth as an individual.

"Sometimes, a little pain is a good sign," he continued. "It means that the tooth is still alive. You know that sailors used to navigate by the stars? Well, we dentists navigate by pain. It tells us where we are in the tooth. If it hurts too much, raise your left hand and I'll stop for a while."

The first two times that I raised my hand, Dr. Mandelbaum stopped drilling for a few seconds, then continued. After the third time, he said, "Andre, I see your hand, but I'm sorry, we have to go on. You're a lucky young man—I think we can save the tooth."

I thought I'd rather have all of my teeth extracted at once, under general anesthesia, and get false teeth. I would never again need any dental work or have to brush my teeth and floss. I could just rinse them out.

When Mandelbaum did give me Novocain, his aim was often a little off. He would numb the tooth next to the one he was working on, or would push in the needle too far, causing a wave of pain.

After five months with Mandelbaum, I got my mother to plead with Doctor Shimkin to take me back.

Now nearly two years later, I still felt grateful to Doctor Shimkin for taking me back. Sitting in his office, re-reading his diplomas and certificates on the wall, I felt reassured.

The only picture he had up was a faded, black-and-white French print of Sainte Apolline, the patron saint of dentists. She hovered in the sky above an idealized young dentist, who was standing with long-handled pincers, about to pull out a tooth from a saintly-looking young woman with her arms bound behind her back to a tree.

Depending on my mood, I viewed the print as confirming either the horrors of dentistry or my good fortune at living in its modern age. I felt lucky to have escaped even the era of the foot-pedal drill, 50 times slower than the electric drill. Doctor

Shimkin told me that, during World War II, several dentists in the army were still using foot-pedal drills. The next patient in line to be treated would pump the pedals for the dentist. If that next patient was tired or sadistic, it was too bad for the patient in the chair. And my mother told me about German dentists who gave Novocain only to girls. The boys were expected to bear the pain, to prepare them for manhood.

Every four months I had my teeth cleaned by Miss Potapov. Slender, with short, dark bangs and sensual lips, Miss Potapov seemed slight, until using the explorer on my teeth. She tugged so hard, I wondered if she was trying to create new cavities for Doctor Shimkin to fill. Then she drove dental floss between my teeth, making my gums bleed. After each session, she would scold me for poor brushing and no flossing. "Unless you practice good home care," she warned, "you'll need deep scaling as an adult."

I resolved to do better. Regular scaling already seemed bad enough.

I suppressed any sexual fantasies about Miss Potapov while she worked in my mouth. If she noticed my excitement, she might take revenge and use the explorer extra zealously, even on my gums.

Only between visits did I let myself imagine a rendezvous with her. I pictured us undressing together in Doctor Shimkin's office after he had left for the day. The possibilities seemed wondrous. Miss Potapov and I might stimulate each other with the air hose and the water squirter, then switch to the electric drill—not with a bur, but a soft toothbrush, feathering it over each other's erogenous areas. We would use heated dental wax, strategically placed, and would trail strands of dental floss over one another from head to foot, closing our eyes to focus on the slightest sensation.

For an interlude, I might put Miss Potapov in the dental chair and use the scaler on her—just hard enough for her to understand what I had felt when she was scraping my teeth, so in the future she would remember that she was dealing with a human being.

I pictured myself in the dental chair, my head tilted back, while Miss Potapov leaned over to kiss me and then straddled me while we made love. I also imagined entering her from behind while she was rummaging in a drawer for which instrument to use next.

But could I do it from behind—would I find the right opening without fumbling? I would use one of Doctor Shimkin's little round magnifying mirrors to locate the right hole, the mirrors that he used to keep track of his progress while drilling.

The one thing that disturbed me about Doctor Shimkin was that, based on the dates of his diplomas, he had to be at least 74. I didn't want to be the patient in whose mouth his drilling hand finally slipped, causing a bad enough injury to lead him to retire. I wished Doctor Shimkin many patients, to spread around the risk.

Chapter Five

THE OPAQUE NIGHTGOWN

> The genital kiss is particularly cal-
> culated to overcome frigidity and fear in
> hitherto inexperienced women.... But—the
> husband must exercise the *greatest gentle-*
> *ness*, the *most delicate reverence!*
> *Ideal Marriage*, p. 174.

MY MOTHER TOOK me to Rogers Peet to buy a new suit for
my Thanksgiving visit to Jessica's. Although I already had a
gray and a blue suit, my mother pointed out that brown was a
fall color and would be good for Thanksgiving.

In the past, I had always wanted to get clothes shopping
over with as quickly as possible.

"It's fine," I would say, after trying on the first jacket or pair
of pants we were shown. "The salesman says it looks good on
me. Let's get it!"

"What else can you show us?" my mother would ask him,
ignoring me. hey would pore through the racks together, gathering up a plethora of suits, all of which I'd have to try on.
Then would come my mother's series of questions to the salesman: "Will it turn baggy?" "Won't it shrink after cleaning?"
And the inevitable, "Are you sure it's not too tight in the
crotch?"

"Mom, it's *fine* in the crotch," I would say to her.

"Would you please make sure," she would ask the salesman, who would reach down and grab the material around my
crotch to show her. "You see, madam, he has lots of room in the

crotch."

That was the past. But now I, too, was seeking the perfect suit. I wanted to look my best for Jessica and her parents—if possible, to look even better than I really did. So I joined in searching through the racks, and I finally settled on a fuzzy textured, dark-brown suit with specks of orange, yellow, and white in it. The specks and fuzziness would help conceal any dandruff I had.

"It's conservative but youthful," said the salesman. "What today's college men are wearing." When he pointed it out, I could see that it looked livelier than a plain brown suit.

This time, my mother's question—"Are the pants too tight in the crotch?"—seemed vital to me, as well. I didn't want to have to reach down and readjust my crotch in front of Jessica or her parents, or have it show any erections I might get.

"Could you make the crotch a little looser?" I asked the tailor, when he was measuring the pants for alterations.

"*Va bené*," he said, smiling. "I understand—a young stallion like yourself." He poked me and winked. "Do you want cuffs, or no cuffs?" he asked.

I had no idea. I had never thought about pants without cuffs.

"Which do you think would look better?" I asked the tailor.

"Well," he said, "the snazzy dressers in Italy are wearing them without cuffs. But for you, I suggest cuffs."

"If you really think so..." I said, disappointed not to be included among the snazzy dressers.

My high school, Mattoon—named for Norman Mattoon Thomas, the six-time Socialist Party candidate for President— had been founded as a progressive school. "We don't teach children *what* to think, but *how* to think," the school catalogue boasted. Yet, a recent magazine article had rated Mattoon among New York's "second-rank schools, euphemistically called 'less competitive.'"

The school's five-story stone building had high, arched windows and ornamental columns encrusted with bird droppings. The interior looked like a cross between a kindergarten and a factory. Several of the walls were painted in industrial salmon; others in bright, kindergarten primary colors—blues, greens, reds, yellows—as if to draw attention away from the school's dilapidated condition. Cigarette butts lined the stairways, and shreds of plaster hung down from the classroom ceilings.

Student paintings decorating the walls of our homeroom illustrated Mattoon's two "themes of the year"—beating swords into ploughshares and U.S.-Soviet Friendship.

The right half of each painting, worked on mainly by the girls, heralded the bright future flowing from disarmament—atomic-powered utilities electrifying remote desert regions; internationally-staffed hospital ships sailing on missions of mercy; masons and welders building Soviet-style cultural centers.

The left half of the paintings, done mainly by the boys, lovingly depicted the outdated legacy of militarism— German V-2 rockets devastating London; American tanks using flame-throwers on Japanese pillboxes; Canadian destroyers dropping depth charges on German submarines that were harassing Allied convoys bound for Murmansk to supply the valiant Soviet people.

Aside from school desegregation in Little Rock, 1957 seemed politically uneventful. The Korean War had ended, America had yet to enter the Vietnam War, and President Eisenhower had been reelected the year before.

Yet, politics was always in the air at Mattoon, where many considered even the Democratic Party right wing. Echoing their parents, about half of the students supported the pro-Soviet Progressive Party, with its presidential candidate, Vincent Hallinan; fewer than half, including myself, favored the Democrats; and only a handful admitted to being Republicans. In weekly meetings of the Current Events Club, whatever the subject discussed, students called each other "Fascist" or "Commie" with predictable regularity.

Student activism ranged from soliciting petitions to clear

Alger Hiss—even after his release from jail—to refusing to take cover under a desk during nuclear air-raid drills. Although I took cover to minimize my risk, I left a finger sticking out to demonstrate social conscience.

My homeroom teacher, Mr. Truewater, was also the biology teacher. He began each school day by leaning back in his chair and asking, "What is life?" then looking around the room, as if hoping someone would tell him. When no one did, he invariably continued, "We cannot know what life is, but we can observe how it manifests itself," and that would lead him into his topic of the day.

I liked Mr. Truewater, but disliked labs. In bio lab I only pretended to dissect frogs or pig embryos, meanwhile tracing out pictures of segmented worms from the textbook, hoping they would make up for my lack of dissections. In chem lab, if the textbook said that a certain mixture would turn orange, I believed it and saw no need to repeat the experiment myself.

In chem class, we learned about co-valent bonds. Two unstable atoms came together and shared an electron between them, forming a new, more stable atom—like sodium and chlorine coming together to form sodium chloride, salt. It was like that with Jessica and me, I thought. Together we formed a more stable atom than either of us alone.

Fortunately, my parents seldom bugged me about my homework. I had shown them an article saying that students left on their own to do their homework got better grades than students whose parents supervised them.

"It's true," my mother agreed. "I've seen it in my own classes."

"Before I could accept that finding," said my father, "I would want to examine the research behind it."

One day in late October, I was visiting my best friend, Brian Larsen, after school. He lived on Riverside Drive, and already in October a chilly wind blew on us as we approached his house. At least I'd have a tail wind on the way back, I consoled myself.

Brian was six feet two, and the star of Mattoon's basketball team. He had short, blond hair that stood up straight, making girls want to run their hands through it. I helped him with his homework. He gave me advice on girls, whom he seemed to handle as smoothly as he sank a swish shot.

Brian called himself a Marxist, but I thought him too cheerful for one. In September he had attended a meeting of the New York Young Socialists Society, and when I asked him how it was, he said, "The dialectic was good, but the chicks were lousy."

We played indoor golf at his place that October afternoon. Brian got out his father's putter and golf balls, and we made three-sided "holes" out of match boxes, which we set up in the hallway, the living room, and Brian's room. While we played, we talked about girls. Brian had been dating Pam Myers from our class, along with a couple of girls from outside of Mattoon.

"If I've been successful with girls," said Brian, "it's because I follow one rule. I don't serve girls, they serve *me*. If you're always serving a girl, she won't respect you. But if *she's* serving you, she feels she's invested in you. It makes her care more. It's simple, man. You just gotta have the right attitude."

It did sound simple, I thought. But Jessica was different. I loved her, I didn't want to play games with her. If we were in love, wouldn't we *each* want to "serve" the other?

Hearing the front door opening, Brian and I raced to put away the putter and the "holes."

"It's nice to see you again, Andre," Brian's mother said to me. She looked about half Brian's size.

"Have you finished your homework yet?" she asked Brian.

"I'll do it tonight," he said.

"No, you'll do it right now! I'm locking you in your room until you finish your homework. And that means you stay there at least two hours. I'm not paying a thousand dollars a year to send you to private school, so you get C's and D's and wind up in some yo-yo college."

She locked Brian into his room and wrote down the time on

65

a piece of paper. Then she told me to help myself to cake and soda and to read or play records "until Brian's finished."

I went into the kitchen and got a glass of cream soda and a piece of dark-chocolate fudge cake and took them into the living room. There I found a book on Japanese atrocities during World War II. I read it in an easy chair while eating my cake and drinking my cream soda.

Scenes from the book haunted me long afterwards. I feared that, if captured by the Japanese, I would have told them anything they wanted to know, to avoid being tortured. But how could I have convinced my fellow prisoners that I *hadn't* talked, unless I had cuts and bruises and broken bones? I wished I'd never read the atrocity book, and I wouldn't have read it if Brian had only done his homework first.

On November 3rd, the Soviet Union launched Sputnik II, over five times as large as Sputnik I, and carrying a dog on board.

Again I feared a nuclear attack. Since the Russians now had built at least two satellites, they could bomb us in different places simultaneously, increasing the risk of New York's being targeted early.

Yet, I felt less afraid than after Sputnik I had been launched. I had Jessica in my life.

I went to a Whelan's drug store to buy a house gift for her parents. For a long time I wavered between a tin of peanut brittle, a box of candied fruit rinds, and a double layer of maple-sugar soldiers with rifles and British Guardsmen's hats. Finally I chose a box of assorted chocolates instead, as more presentable. The saleslady clinched it for me by saying, "Our two-pound assortment is the ideal gift for a young man to bring when visiting."

Along with the chocolates for Jessica's parents, I bought a small chocolate turkey for myself. *Ideal Marriage* said that "the genital kiss is particularly calculated to overcome frigidity and fear in hitherto inexperienced women." But "the husband must exercise the *greatest gentleness*, the *most delicate reverence!*"

Alone late at night, I practiced on the turkey's ridged comb, imagining it a clitoris that I was arousing with my tongue. Then after wearing down the comb, I practiced on the turkey's narrow head. While I hardly thought I'd get to lick Jessica's clitoris over Thanksgiving, I wanted to be prepared just in case. Or if not with Jessica, then with someone else in the future.

On Tuesday, November 26, the day before leaving for Jessica's, I skimmed through *Ideal Marriage*, looking for last-minute tips. "The lightest touches are the most effective," said a passage on page 162. I practiced on my arms, chest, and nipples, trying to arouse myself with light touches. Another passage said that the erogenous zones included not only the genitals and anus, but also the mouth, ears, nose, and the "lateral portions of the eye-sockets." If only I could remember it all when I was with Jessica.

That night I dreamt that I was standing outdoors near a well, kissing a red-headed girl in a green dress. Suddenly I was inside her, moving back and forth. We were actually making love.

On awakening at three in the morning, I felt desolate. It had been only a dream. I was still a virgin.

The dream had been so vivid. One minute the girl and I had been standing near the well, kissing; in the next we were making love. It had all seemed natural and easy, no fumbling with anything. I was simply there, inside her. I couldn't remember whether we had made love standing up or lying down. Nor could I place the girl. She wasn't Jessica, but she had seemed familiar.

I went back to sleep, hoping the dream would come back. Next time I would pay close attention and try to learn from it. I wanted to find out all the steps on the way that had led up to our making love. Then I could apply them with Jessica. Unfortunately, the dream didn't come back.

The next morning's paper announced that President Eisenhower had suffered a "mild stroke," but was improving. I felt relieved once my train to Boston had left New York. If the

Russians attacked now—figuring that Eisenhower's stroke had weakened America—I would at least have seen Jessica one more time.

My Thanksgiving with her was the best Thanksgiving I could remember. She and her parents picked me up at the train station in Boston and welcomed me warmly. Jessica gave me a quick, reassuring kiss. Her father shook hands and thanked me for coming. Her mother embraced me and almost wouldn't let go.

Even their house appealed to me—its stairway with a wooden banister connecting the two floors, its enclosed sun porch overlooking a tree-filled back yard, and its comfortably-furnished living room with a fire burning in the fireplace and a 3½-pound brook trout mounted on the wall.

My own living room at home seemed austere by comparison. The chairs and couches hugged the walls, so everyone looked out into space, like panelists addressing a distant audience. Although our fireplace worked, we couldn't use it: My parents feared that the smoke would stain the paintings on the walls—mostly dark Old Masters, with plump men, chubby babies, and sexless women.

Jessica's mother reminded me over dinner to use their first names—"I'm Maud and he's Oliver." But I felt embarrassed to do so. It seemed rude. I couldn't make myself say, "Oliver, would you please pass the pot roast?" I just looked at him, instead, and asked for "a little more pot roast," without saying his name.

After dinner we played Monopoly on a coffee table in front of the fireplace. Jessica's parents didn't let Eisenhower's stroke dampen the mood. We laughed over ludicrous property-trade offers—a "Get out of Jail Free" card and the two utilities for the four railroads—and we passed around the chocolates I had brought as a house gift.

Partway through the game, Jessica's mother came over and pinched my cheeks. "Forgive me, I can't help it," she said. "You're so cute, Andre. Do you know how special we think you are?"

"Well, thank you. I, I think you're special, too." I felt warm and appreciated. But when Jessica's mother kept on peering into my eyes, I began to feel uneasy.

Jessica's parents went to bed around ten. I put two more logs on the fire and sat down next to Jessica on the couch, facing it.

At last we were alone and with no time pressure, unlike when we had kissed outside her hotel room in New York.

"I like looking at fires," I said, taking Jessica's hand in mine."

"I love looking at fires," she said. (I envied her use of superlatives and vowed to use them more, myself.) "When I watch the flames dancing, I always imagine something romantic will happen in my life, someday. Then I go upstairs and do my homework, while keeping that romantic glow from the fire."

"Jessica, that's beautiful!" I said. "Like *you*." I kissed her and she kissed me back.

"I'm kissing the girl I love," I told myself. I wanted to focus on every aspect of the kiss to re-live them all later—her cool hand caressing the back of my neck, her soft lips moving along mine, even her occasional snorts when clearing her nose. They were all part of my Jessica.

Once, I thought I felt her tongue in my mouth, but so lightly I might have imagined it. I touched my own tongue to her lips, but didn't push through them in case I'd been mistaken and it offended her.

"Is that your father's trout on the wall?" I asked, thinking I should say something.

"Don't talk!" Jessica pressed two fingers against my lips.

In between kisses, I caressed Jessica, staying above the waist and avoiding her breasts, afraid I might spoil things by one bad mistake.

I kept caressing her along the same route, down and up each arm, circling her neck, and—recalling *Ideal Marriage*'s instruc-

69

tions—around her mouth, nose, and ears, and what I thought were the "lateral portions" of her eye sockets.

After a while, I sensed my caresses becoming boring. Like running my electric trains on only the small, inner loop, never the large, outer one. I began to wish that Jessica had a curfew.

When the clock chimed eleven, she said, "Uh, oh, bedtime. I have to help Mom prepare the Thanksgiving dinner tomorrow. You can help, too, but only if you want to."

"I *do*," I said, wanting to make up for my boring caresses.

Jessica gave me a final kiss and hurried up the stairs.

"Until tomorrow, adieu," she said, waving from the second-floor balcony.

"Adieu, sweet lady, 'till the morrow." I blew her a kiss, hoping I was striking a light, but courtly pose.

I slept in her brother's room. He was in Grenoble on a junior-year-of-college-abroad program.

The room exuded warmth. It had walls and ceiling of pine. A bookcase occupied the end wall facing the windows; a bed ran along one side wall, underneath a Princeton pennant; a poster of Audrey Hepburn hung on the opposite wall.

I held out my hands toward the poster palms upward and shrugged.

"I'm sorry, Audrey," I said. "It's too late. My heart's already taken."

Jessica and I shared a common bathroom that separated our rooms. Although a full set of towels—hand towel, face towel, and bath towel—had been laid out for me, I used only the bath towel, to minimize the laundry I created.

Sharing a bathroom with Jessica felt intimate—her pale-pink toothbrush in one glass, my dark-blue toothbrush in the other. I imagined it a preview of future together. When we were married, though, we might keep our toothbrushes in the same glass.

I put my toothbrush in Jessica's glass for a few moments, to look at the brushes side by side. But I kept their bristles from touching, thinking that would violate Jessica's privacy. I returned my toothbrush to my own glass before leaving the bathroom.

Back in my room, I felt too excited to fall asleep right away. Lying in bed, I made imaginary designs on the ceiling by connecting the knotholes in the pine boards. Then I got up and went to the bookcase and, after considering a collection of short stories and a book on happiness by Bertrand Russell, I finally chose *Economics*, a textbook by Paul Samuelson, and took it back to bed with me.

I had never read any economics before. In the historical section, I learned about European mercantilism versus British laissez-faire; Adam Smith's theory that the "invisible hand" of the marketplace made individuals' pursuit of their own self-interest serve the common good, as well; and the physiocrats' belief that real wealth grew only from agriculture, where human beings mixed their labor with that of God, who had created the land. Then I jumped ahead to modern capitalist theory, demonstrating how, in micro-economics, wages, prices, and interest rates mutually adjusted until supply and demand reached equilibrium.

I sensed a new world opening up for me. Through reading *Economics*, I was starting to prepare for Jessica's and my future together.

At two a.m., I put down the book, turned out my bedside light, and opened my door an inch. If Jessica came to my room during the night, she shouldn't have to risk making noise opening the door. Although the chance of her coming to my room was tiny, it was greater than zero. To me, that was the wonderful thing about probability. Even the most improbable event had at least *some* chance of occurring.

If Jessica did come to my room, I wouldn't try to make love with her. I would just hold her close to me in bed and ask her to marry me and tell her that I was already laying the groundwork to be able to support her. I would even keep my pajama bottoms on all night, with the snaps shut. I realized that the snaps were too far apart to offer much protection, but my character would protect her.

Of course, if *Jessica* wanted to make love, I would agree.

Afterwards, I would ask her again to marry me, so she'd know I'd been serious, not just out to sleep with her.

On Thanksgiving morning I helped Jessica and her parents prepare the dinner. I chopped onions for the stuffing, peeled chestnuts after they'd cooled barely enough to touch, and snapped the ends off a seemingly endless supply of string beans, all the while feeling happy inside, as if already part of the family.

Jessica's mother kept thanking me for helping, practically for each bean I snapped.

"Have you any plans to come to New York again?" I asked her, to make conversation.

"Do you mean metaphorically or physically?" she said, and I regretted having asked.

"I'm often in New York metaphorically," she continued. "Even when I'm in Concord physically. I literally couldn't live without metaphor. I think it reveals life, and vice versa. Do you agree, Andre?" She stared at me.

"I do," I said, as if I'd understood what she was talking about. "How long have you lived in Concord?" I asked, searching for a safer subject.

"For me it's not how long I live in a place," she said, "but what I learn about myself from living there."

"Don't let my mother get to you," Jessica said to me later, when her parents had driven off to buy some more apple cider. Jessica and I were still in the kitchen, washing up the bowls and other implements from the morning's food preparation. I liked her family's mounted, wooden knife-holder with slots for the various-size knives. At home, we stashed all the knives in the same drawer, then had to hunt among them.

"I know my mother runs on and on," Jessica continued. "Just give me the short version," I tell her. But she's a warm person underneath."

"I can see that about her," I said, recalling her hugs and compliments. "But isn't it great that you recognize that she runs

72

on and on? It means you won't repeat it yourself. I've been trying to learn from observing my parents, too."

"Andre, there something I want to ask you. But you have to promise me, you'll feel free to say no."

"I promise."

"Andre, would you like to go to my spring prom with me? It's not till the third Saturday in May. So there's no hurry. You've plenty of time to think about it."

"I'd love to go with you," I said. "I don't need to think about it." I went up to Jessica and kissed her. But I kept the kiss short. Her parents might return any moment, and it seemed strange to be kissing in the kitchen, in daylight.

I felt relieved. My boring caresses hadn't ruined things for me with Jessica after all. Emboldened by her inviting me to her prom, I asked her for a picture of herself that I could keep in my wallet.

She gave me a black-and-white snapshot of her in a white shirt with rolled-up sleeves. She was standing in front of a church, looking so sweet and mischievous that I fell in love with the picture itself.

Both sets of Jessica's grandparents had been invited for Thanksgiving, along with a French banker colleague of Jessica's father and the banker's slim, elegant wife. She told me that she and her husband would be "ravished" to have me stay with them in Paris. I could help their 15-year-old daughter with her English.

The Thanksgiving turkey was delicious. The stuffing contained no questionable innards, and even the string beans tasted good to me. They were bright green, enlivened with butter, and not overcooked, unlike the watery, olive-green string beans at school lunches.

"Would you please pass the cranberry jelly?" I asked Jessica's mother at one point.

She started to pass it to me, then stopped mid-way. Holding the jelly dish up high, she tapped on it with a spoon for silence.

"Have I told you about the history of my cranberry jelly?" she addressed the whole table. "It's become a family legend. I first tasted it at a hotel that my Olie and I were staying at in Maine, in Prout's Neck. As soon as I tasted their jelly, well, those of you who know me can imagine what I thought. I thought, why not make ..."

I pondered my dilemma. Should I eat my turkey warm but without cranberry jelly, or wait for the jelly while the turkey cooled off? While debating it, I ate two brussels sprouts for politeness and found the jelly passed to me at last.

Conversation and banter flowed freely at dinner. Two wines were served—a cabernet sauvignon in a large glass and an Alsatian riesling in a smaller, narrower glass—and Jessica's father went around refilling glasses, even Jessica's and mine, although we were legally under age. I compared dinners at my own home, where my father poured the wine into tiny sherry glasses, with one bottle serving six and a little left over for the maid.

After the guests left, Jessica and her mother did the dishes, leaving me alone with her father. I liked him. He seemed to have her mother's warmth, but without her babbling.

"That's quite a trout you've got on the wall," I said to him. "It's bigger than any I've ever caught." I wanted to let him know that I shared his interest in fishing.

He took me up to his study in the attic and showed me his fly-tying equipment—his bench and vice, wing and neck feathers, rabbit fur and peacock hurl. Still floating from the wine at dinner, I felt as if I was talking with him fisherman to fisherman. He spoke of "marrying the wings" on a Parmacheene Belle—stroking adjacent pieces of red and white wing feathers together until they adhered to each other and became one. I tried to apply the idea to Jessica and me, imagining us stroking each other until we merged into one person.

In bed later I propped up Jessica's picture so I could see it while lying on my pillow. What a luxury awaited me, I thought, to look at her picture every night before falling asleep and every morning on awakening.

I imagined Jessica sitting at her desk after we were married, writing our social correspondence. "My husband and I are pleased to accept your gracious invitation to ...." One small benefit of being married to her—along with all the important things—was that she would write our thank-you notes. "Your gift was perfect! How did you know that Andre and I are wild about springer spaniel prints?"

"Mom and Dad put no pressure on me about college," Jessica said to me the next morning. We were walking together across the Concord River, on the "rude bridge that arched the flood." The sun was shining, the water sparkling, and the temperature over 60 degrees. Surely, God was smiling on us as a couple.

"Any college I choose is fine with them," Jessica continued. "'Be whatever you want,' they tell me. But how can I tell them my real ambition is just to be average?

"Maybe I *will* become a doctor," she said, "like my mother thinks. But I could also imagine being a bank teller. Wouldn't it be fascinating to watch people's faces when they deposit their money, or when they withdraw it?"

Jessica's wish to be average only proved her sincerity, I thought. She wasn't putting on airs.

"I think I'd like being average," she said. "There's this Italian boy at school, Marco. He told me that his uncle goes to Germany for six months every year to work for the German telephone company. Then he comes back to Italy, and he lies in the sun and makes love for six months. He knows that when his money runs out the German phone company will still be there. Does that sound terrible to you?"

"No, it sounds good. It sounds *great*."

"You know what I'd really like?" said Jessica. "I would like, if I get married someday, to try to make my marriage into a work of art. That would be more important to me than being famous or anything. You must think I'm being naive?"

"Jessica, I think it's a *beautiful* idea." Jessica shared my dream! "It's exactly what I want, too." I wanted to propose to her on the spot, but she might think I was rushing things.

"Oh, well." Jessica laughed. "I'll probably get more realistic when I grow up."

"No, it *is* realistic," I insisted. "I've started reading on economics, to make it realistic, so it's not just a dream. Jessica, it can work if we always keep it in mind. Shall we pledge ourselves never to forget it, no matter what?"

"Can't we just say that we'll do our best and leave it at that?"

"Of course," I said, feeling my happiness slipping away. Jessica was taking marriage as a work of art too lightly, like some notion she was trying out.

"Sure, it's a nice thought," she said. "If I'm lucky, maybe I'll realize it someday. Or I won't and it'll be no big deal."

My cloud lifted during lunch of a cold turkey wing with crispy skin. It struck me that Jessica hadn't been rejecting me. She just wasn't ready to get engaged yet. After all, we had only seen each other on two weekends.

For me it was simple. I loved Jessica. I knew I'd never find any other girl as good for me. Why couldn't it be clear for her, too? We would save a lot of time.

That evening, my last at Jessica's, I saw her walking to the bathroom in her nightgown. It was high-necked and opaque, with little flowers and sheep on it, as innocent as the wallpaper in a child's bedroom. But it was a nightgown with Jessica in it.

I recalled the Pullman-car brochures I had seen on night trains. The brochures showed a man and a woman in a compartment—the man in pajamas, brushing his teeth over a small sink; the woman in a nightgown, already in the lower berth. Previously I had looked at those brochures wistfully, imagining myself as the man and various girls at school as the woman. Now I pictured Jessica as the woman.

I wondered when would be the best time to propose to her. While I didn't want to press her, I'd read that a man's sexual peak was in his teens. I didn't want to wait so long that our marriage would be all decline.

Chapter Six

THE WAGES OF SIN

So long as anyone loves ardently with
both soul and senses, the mind is so pervaded
by the image of the beloved, that the lover
remains monogamous in essentials ....
Ideal Marriage, page. 17.

BACK IN NEW YORK, I smiled at couples on the street holding hands. I wanted to go up to them and explain that we shared
a common bond. I was in love, too.

What did it matter that I was separated from my beloved by
some 200 miles? That was nothing, compared with couples
divided by war, or by one of them living in the Soviet Union,
unable to get out, or by the husband or wife serving a prison
term, especially if innocent.

I would see Jessica again in only five months, for her spring
prom. Meanwhile, I would become more observant of my sur-
roundings, looking for things to describe to her. I would be like
a dachshund I had seen, walking along the street, head down,
yet noticing a sparrow 40 feet overhead.

I bought my own copy of *Economics* and alternated
between reading it and *Ideal Marriage* in whatever spare time I
had after doing my schoolwork.

In *Economics* I was intrigued by the luxury demand curve.
Unlike the usual demand curve, where sales dropped as prices
rose, with certain luxury items—fancy cars, Italian shoes, Park
Avenue doctors—sales went up as prices rose. Apparently,
higher prices were associated with greater quality and status.

"My doctor costs me an arm and a leg, but he's worth it," said a friend of my parents. "He's the top man in the field."

I imagined owning a store and announcing price increases, instead of sales, leading customers to buy before prices rose even more.

In *Ideal Marriage* I read that, "if both partners 'meet each other half-way,' are attentive, and adaptable to one another's needs . and by a *culture of erotic technique* beyond all present marital usage . happiness is attained and preserved in the ideal marriage."

I would meet Jessica at least half way and always be attentive to her needs, and *Ideal Marriage* would teach me the "culture of erotic technique."

Life seemed perfect. The girl I wanted to marry had invited me to her spring prom, her biggest event of the year. I sensed that I was entering into the happiest period I'd ever known.

Yet, I also feared death, not only from a nuclear attack, but even from old age after a long life.

I imagined turning 65 and feeling that I'd arrived there in a flash, as if my whole life had been telescoped into a few years. Suddenly, I would find myself in my grandparents' generation. I would fear falling asleep each night, lest it be my last. Nor could I talk about death with my parents. Since they were probably closer to it than I was, I didn't want to frighten them by bringing it up. My only hope lay in science's finding a cure for mortality before I died.

I thought again about *The Amboy Dukes*, the novel of the teenage boy who winds up in the electric chair for murder. I imagined that, if I were facing execution, I would try to slow down time by savoring the hours and minutes of life I had left— each meal I ate, each glimpse of the sky and touch of my prison pillow. Then why not do the same in my own life, even without facing imminent death? By living each moment fully, I might make my life seem to stretch out infinitely, especially after marrying Jessica. In a normal lifetime, I calculated, I would have thousands of nights with her, hundreds of thousands of hours, and millions of minutes.

The biggest event of the year for our junior class was the 10-day trip in April by chartered bus. The official purpose of the trip was to study American historical sites—Gettysburg, Washington's crossing of the Delaware, Lincoln's log cabin in Kentucky. The students' goals were sex, romance, and various combinations of the two.

Already in early December, Adrienne Hart and Pam Myers, the leaders of the two rival cliques of junior girls, had drawn up separate lists of who would be sitting with whom on the bus. Since after meeting Jessica, I had stopped dating anyone else, both lists showed me as "Available for leftover girls"—any of the five extra girls in the class.

Each student had to earn $100 for the trip. I "earned" $19.43 simply by looking for money. When walking on the street, I stayed near the curb, searching for coins that had fallen when people got out of their cars. Even on days when I found nothing, just looking for money made walking exciting.

I also branched out into hotel lobbies—theBiltmore, the Roosevelt, the Waldorf. Dressed in a suit and tie, I would sit in the lobby reading, as if waiting for one of the hotel guests. Whenever someone got up from a chair or sofa, I would take that person's place and check for fallen coins, surreptitiously, in case a hotel detective was watching. Since hotel furniture was generally upholstered and the floors carpeted, even quarters and half-dollars might fall out of pockets without the person noticing.

The bulk of my trip money I earned working at Davega's sporting goods store over Christmas vacation. I received $5.50 a day, plus a six per cent commission on sales. I enjoyed calculating my commission on even the smallest sales—1½ cents on a 25-cent Spaldeen ball, 2.3 cents on a 39-cent set of jacks.

When I was about to sell my first expensive item, a Jack Kramer Autograph tennis racket, one of the regular salesmen glided over and smiled. "I'll handle this one, young man," he said, and took the sale away.

I resolved it would never happen again. I wouldn't do the work and have another salesman get the commission.

From then on, whenever a customer asked about an expensive item, I said, "I would be glad to help you, but would you prefer one of our older salesmen?" I always said, *older*, rather than *more experienced*, to avoid undermining myself.

If the customer preferred an "older" salesman, I handed over the sale immediately, before putting any work into it. But if the customer declined my offer, as many did, and then a regular salesman tried to take over, the customer usually insisted on staying with me.

One day, a woman asked me for ice skates for her eight-year-old daughter. After I found a pair in the right size and laced them up on the girl, her mother asked, "Are you sure these are on the right feet?"

"Yes," I said. "They just feel tight until they get broken in." I recalled my mother's telling me that about shoes.

"No!" cried the girl's mother. "These are on the wrong feet. Are you blind? If my daughter wears them, it's her *legs* that'll get 'broken in.'"

My stomach sank. The woman was right. Both toes curved in the same direction. How could I have missed it?

"I'm terribly sorry," I said, feeling panicky. "I'm new here. I've never sold skates before." Why had I ever argued with her?

"Well, I should report you," said the woman. "But you *did* apologize. Maybe I'll give you a break, just because I'm a nice person."

"Thank you," I said. "Thank you very, very, very much."

"Frankly, I have to tell you, it disturbs me to think of you getting a commission on the ice skates, when you could have broken my daughter's legs. Doesn't that seem wrong to you?"

"You're right. I'll be glad to give up my commission. In fact, I insist on it." I didn't want her to change her mind and report me. "I'll pay you the six per cent, myself, because I have to write up the sales slip for the full price."

"No," she said, "just give me five per cent. I want you to have something for doing the right thing in the end."

I felt lucky to get off that easy. No one would learn of my mistake, and I would even get 12 cents commission. Not bad for having laced up the skates on the wrong feet.

My love for Jessica heightened my every day and night. In the early mornings, I lay in bed listening to the pile drivers on the building site across from my window and imagining they were a steam engine, pulling a train on which Jessica and I were riding. I pictured us riding the Empire State Express or the Twentieth Century Limited. We would sit in the streamliner's rounded observation car, looking out the back, continuing to hold hands in it at night after the lights had been turned out.

On rainy days I held only half of my umbrella over me, preparing for holding the other half over Jessica. In restaurants I watched couples leaning across the table toward each other with adoring looks, and I felt I was sharing in their happiness.

At class parties, I didn't envy the boys who had girlfriends with them. Looking at couples petting in the semi-darkened living room—the party-giver's parents having insisted that a hallway light remain on—I noticed that, whenever a boy's hand touched a girl's breasts, the boy kissed her at the same time. Was it to distract her from what he was doing, I wondered, or to demonstrate that his feelings for her meant more to him than touching her breasts?

At Mattoon's February winter dance, I danced a few times with Pam Myers, whom Brian was still dating. Both of them were tall and blond—Brian medium blond, Pam pale blonde. She had a pretty face and talked quietly and demurely, belying her sharpness. I liked her a lot.

During one dance, I suddenly sensed that the rhythm had changed. It now seemed kind of Latin, but different from a rhumba.

"What dance is this?" I asked Pam.

"Why do you care?" she said, quietly. "You dance the same step to everything."

I was startled. I had thought I'd been varying my steps,

making subtle distinctions according to the beat and speed of the music. Then I realized that Pam was right. I had been doing mostly the two-step, speeding it up on lively numbers and shifting to a one-step with random staccato movements for Latin music.

Now I feared Jessica's prom. My lousy dancing would embarrass her in front of her friends.

I decided to take dance lessons. An ad for a dance studio on East 86th Street offered an "introductory half-hour lesson" for two dollars.

The "studio" was a room in a fourth-floor walk-up. It was bare, except for two folding chairs and a phonograph on a table. The teacher, Señora Alvarez from the Dominican Republic, was tall and slim, with shiny black hair that tumbled down on one side and was swept up on the other and held in place with a comb, except for a series of tendrils curling around her cheek and ear. She wore a silvery scoop-necked blouse and a chartreuse wraparound skirt and looked to me like the kind of older woman I had read about in stories set in Europe who initiates the teenage boy into sex.

"This will be our secret, Andre. You must promise not to tell your mama or papa. They would not understand and it would spoil everything. Can I trust you, my Andrelito?" "I swear it, Señora!" "You may call me Rosaria." I looked away, lest she could read my thoughts.

"First, we will dance," said Señora Alvarez. "Then we will evaluate for which series you should take." She put on a record that started with a slow dance.

I danced stiffly, barely touching her waist to conceal my excitement. Then the music switched to a lindy, a rumba, and a waltz, and I forgot any sexual thoughts in struggling to adjust to the rhythms. I shifted arbitrarily between a one-step and a two-step, mixing them together in the waltz and snapping my fingers during the lindy.

At the end of the half hour, Señora Alvarez said to me, "You have a good potential. I propose to you our Series One, in which you are learning the fundamentals of ballroom dancing.

Six lessons for twenty-three dollars, a one-dollar saving from the normal price of four dollars a lesson."

Over the next six weeks, I took a lesson every Saturday morning. In between, I imagined myself a superb dancer, leading Señora Alvarez, as well as Jessica, through a whirlwind of dips, turns, and flourishes, to heights neither had ever before experienced.

The actual lessons went differently. I kept repeating the most basic steps, counting to myself and regretting that the floor-length mirrors on the walls kept me from resting whenever Señora Alvarez danced with her back to me.

I tried it once and she caught me. "Have you no shame, Señor Andre? What would say the señoritas?"

"The señoritas would never know," I defended myself. "There aren't all those mirrors at the dances I go to."

"Ha! *You* would know. You would say, 'Señora Alvarez has not taught me correctly.'"

After my sixth and final lesson, Señora Alvarez announced, "Today, you have completed Series One. You have done well, for your capabilities. I now propose to you Series Two, which we call 'Intermediate Level and Reinforcement of the Fundamentals'"

I declined. Whatever Señora Alvarez said, I knew that I hadn't learned Series One. All I could remember was the basic box step and how to start off a dance with a sweeping glide. Anyway, only five weeks remained before Jessica's prom, and for ten days of that time I would be away on my junior-class trip.

Franklin Dubois was short and fat and getting "A's" in every course but chemistry. He shook his fist under the nose of the chemistry teacher, who'd given him a "B."

"You rotten bastard!" Franklin yelled at the teacher in front of the class. "God damn you, you bastard!" I covered my mouth and looked down to avoid grinning. Compared with Franklin at least, I felt I was suavity itself.

Franklin and I shared two things—doing our homework together and analyzing love and marriage.

Franklin maintained that, if a boy and girl were both virgins when they married, it would make their marriage more special. "Like going to Times Square on a Saturday night with your best girl when it's all lit up. You hold hands with her, and you look at all the lights on Broadway, and you think how really swell she is."

I said that, on the contrary, I owed it to my wife *not* to be a virgin. *Ideal Marriage* said that married men "are naturally educators and initiators of their wives in sexual matters." But how could I educate and initiate my wife into sex if I was still a virgin and was worried about such hazards I had read of, as impotence, premature ejaculation, or urinary reflex under stress?

I assumed that my wife would be a virgin. "It'll be okay if she's not," I told Franklin. "Provided she isn't promiscuous." (Promiscuity, I had read, could reflect deep-seated problems, making marriage more risky.) Either way *I* should be experienced. If my wife was a virgin, I'd need experience to know how to guide her. If she wasn't, I'd need it to keep up with her.

When spring arrived, I grew restless. Sex seemed to be everywhere. Necklines fell. Dresses got brighter and bolder, with tantalizing armholes. Bare midriffs appeared and tank tops that exposed a girl's entire side, including parts of her bra.

Spring was the season of romance on the rebound, when boys who were dropped by a girlfriend went in search of "new flesh," and girls who were dropped by a boyfriend looked for another "mature enough to take responsibility."

"The wages of sin are death," proclaimed a large sign visible from afar on Upper Broadway. "So are the wages of life," I thought.

At a party two weeks before our class trip, I danced with Lucy Trotter, a transfer student from Fayetteville, North Carolina. Her thin lips and pasty skin intrigued me. Maybe they

86

hid unexpected sensuality, much as I wondered about nuns's faces when I peered at them for hints of desire. And Lucy wore her hair in ringlets, which I associated with lustfulness.

While dancing with Lucy, I caressed her back with my fingertips, just by varying their pressure. She moved in closer to me in response. I sensed that Lucy would go out with me if I asked her. But I knew that she'd recently had two dates with Franklin, and the code among boys prohibited stealing a friend's girl, however distant the friend.

I assumed that she would sit with Franklin on the bus during the class trip. In fact, I knew that he was lugging along an anthology of *Immortal Poetry* for them to read from to each other.

So I was surprised on the day we left to see Lucy walk right past Franklin on the bus and sit down next to one of the "leftover" girls.

Everything looked magical to me out the bus window as we drove through New Jersey that first evening in early twilight. Even an insurance-agency lawn sparkled in a luminescent green, and the oranges and blues of sunset, set against white clouds—puffy in the foreground, wispy in the distance— seemed unnaturally beautiful, as if photographed through a filter, or belonging to a more exotic locale than New Jersey.

We stayed that night at Free Acres, a single-tax colony in New Jersey with a history of attracting New York left-wingers. It had been founded on the idea of the Socialist Henry George that people should pay only one tax for everything.

The next morning we visited Independence Hall in Philadelphia, where Franklin tried to test the local guide by asking a series of questions about the least-known members of the Continental Congress.

Mr. Carlin, our history teacher, intervened. "Franklin is a wise guy," he said to the class, "because, unlike Socrates, he hasn't yet learned to love wisdom."

On the fifth evening, after we'd visited Lincoln's log cabin in Hodgenville, Kentucky, Lucy sat next to me on the bus.

"I have totally broken off with Franklin," she declared. She said that she had sat with him during the previous two days out of guilt at having previously ignored him.

"It was wicked wrong of me ever to date him," she said. "I only did it as an experiment—to try out my belief that even the dullest person has interesting qualities, if you search for them."

The immediate cause of the break, she said, was a pin that Franklin had made in crafts class and had given her that morning. It was diamond shaped, about two and a half inches long, and had the letter "P," for the Philadelphia Phillies, Franklin's favorite baseball team, mounted in red felt on a silver-plated copper base.

"It's the ugliest piece of jewelry I've ever seen," said Lucy. "It feels like it weighs ten pounds. As soon as Franklin gave it to me, I knew I had to break up with him. That pin was the final test. I mean, if I'd really cared for Franklin, I would have worn it anyway." Lucy put a hand on top of mine.

I laughed and put my other hand on top of hers, forming a sandwich with her hand in the middle.

"Lucy, I don't want to come between you and Franklin," I said. Not that I minded, but I wanted to feel blameless and to show concern.

"Don't worry, you're *not*," said Lucy, "Cross my heart."

I felt happy that Lucy was sitting with me, that she'd picked me over Franklin. I wanted to put my arm around her, but in a way that seemed natural.

"Did you like the food at the diner tonight?" I asked.

"I did," she said. "And the waitress seemed very genuine. What did you order?—I didn't notice."

"The chicken," I said, sliding an arm around her. "The batter-fried chicken with mashed potatoes and corn. And the cole slaw, instead of salad. How about you?" I squeezed her toward me.

"The single lamb chop." She laid her head on my shoulder.

"What vegetables did it come with?" I asked, my curiosity momentarily overriding desire.

"Peas. It came with peas."

I kissed her while her mouth was still open from saying,

"Peas."

She kissed me back strongly, her breath hot around my face. Then we snuggled awhile, cheek to cheek, alternately kissing and letting the motion of the bus throw us together and apart. Out the window I saw the lights of a passenger train running parallel to us. I savored the combination—caressing Lucy and watching the train.

She opened two of my shirt buttons and moved her fingers along my chest. Then she took my hand and placed it under her sweater and over her bra. I instantly grew excited. No girl had ever placed my hand right on her bra before.

Suddenly, Lucy' face was moving back and forth across mine. She was kissing me continuously and quivering, her hand clutching at my chest. "Kiss me, kiss me, kiss me," she kept saying, as if running on automatic. Then she reached down and grabbed at my crotch.

It was the most exciting moment of my life, and also the most dangerous. Her uncontrolled grabbing and squeezing could injure me. And others might see us.

I lifted up her hand and kissed it as if out of love. Then I took her face in my hands and looked into her eyes.

"Lucy, I love being with you," I said. It was the closest I could come to saying, "I love you," without lying.

If only we could be alone somewhere, I would lose my virginity. It was within reach.

I pushed away the thought that I was betraying Jessica, vowing to think about it later as a non-virgin, when I could be more objective.

I needed to find somewhere with enough privacy for Lucy and me to make love. Certainly not the youth hostels that we had been staying in on the trip. The girls slept in one large room, the boys in another. Maybe we could sneak out at night to the woods or a field.

Now I wished I had bought some condoms in New York before leaving. I had read that in many states they could be sold only as "disease preventives," and I felt embarrassed about asking a drug-store clerk for a box of "disease preventives." But I would do it anyway. It was part of being a man.

"Thank you," said Lucy, breaking into my thoughts.

"You're welcome," I said. For what?"

"For being such a sweetie pie. You saw that my body was running away from my mind, and you didn't take advantage. That meant a lot to me." She touched my cheek. "I want to mean a lot to you, too."

"You do," I said. "You mean a great deal to me." I kissed her again, trying to get back to where we'd been.

Lucy kissed me quickly, then pushed me away.

"I'm sorry," she said. "Here we haven't even had a date yet, and I'm acting as if we're practically engaged. I feel ashamed of myself, and ever so foolish."

"Oh, Lucy, let's be foolish together. I *love* you." I couldn't let my chance slip away now.

"I hope you'll *come* to love me, Andre. You don't know me yet. Now, be honest, lambie pie—isn't it lust you're expressing, not love? Not that there's anything wrong with lust. I love it myself."

Lucy patted my hand. "I feel I can trust you," she said. Am I right?"

"Mmm," I said, regretting that I'd calmed her down when she'd turned wild. She could have sat on my lap and we could have done it in the dark before anyone noticed.

"Andre, what do you mean, 'Mmm'? Can't you say, 'Yes, Lucy, you can trust me'? I heard that you're seeing a girl in Boston. Is it true?"

I wanted time to think, but hesitation would seem like an admission.

"Actually, she's not in Boston," I said. "She's in Concord. And I only saw her twice. You had two dates with Franklin."

"Andre, I wasn't accusing you. I just wanted to know. If we are going to have a relationship, we have to be utterly honest with each other. Don't you agree?"

"I do," I said, feeling I had no choice in my answer and resenting it.

"For the rest of the trip," she said, "shall we just sit togeth-

90

er and hold hands and learn all about each other?"

"Lucy, I have a different idea." I felt desperate.

"Tell me."

"I'm not sure I can." I wanted to get permission ahead of time.

"Lambie pie, you can tell me anything at all. I insist on it."

"Okay, if you want me to be completely honest—"

"You know I do."

"Well then, what I honestly want," I said, "is .. is to do it the other way around."

"The other way around?"

"That we sleep together *now*, as soon as we get a chance. And then when we get back, we start dating. Oh, Lucy, wouldn't it be wonderful to go out on dates after we'd already slept together? Then it wouldn't be a question anymore. We could enjoy dating without any tension over it."

"Andre, I truly appreciate your telling me what's on your mind. I know that you're very sincere. Shall I be honest with you, too?"

"Of course."

"Don't get me wrong," said Lucy, "I'm not a virgin. She laughed. "I can't even be friends with virgins. We have nothing in common. But there's one thing my mother's right about— Don't sleep with a boy, if you want him to marry you. I'm not saying I want to marry you, Andre, but I could *imagine* it. That's why I won't sleep with you, although I know we would make beautiful love together. You should consider it a compliment."

"Thank you ... I guess."

I felt flattered that Lucy might want to marry me. It was the first proposal I'd ever received. But did I want to marry a girl who would sleep with me only if she didn't want to marry me? It seemed too calculating.

"Lucy," I said, an idea coming to me, "are you saying that you'd sleep with me if you knew you didn't want to marry me?"

"Yes, I would. Your innocent little baby face excites me."

"Well, what if I told you I wouldn't marry you, whether or

91

not we slept together? Then would you sleep with me, since you'd know there was no chance of marrying me?"

"No, I would know you were only saying you wouldn't marry me to get me to sleep with you."

For the rest of the trip I regretted having taken Lucy's hand off my groin. It had taught me a lesson. The next time an opportunity came along, I'd take it first and reflect on it later.

Maybe things had turned out for the best, I told myself. This way, I remained faithful to Jessica. I had nothing to hide from her. No, I thought, ruefully—I would rather have made love and concealed it. I was used to keeping secrets.

Chapter Seven

BORN AGAIN AGAIN

He who cannot embrace a woman
with dominant virility will be neither
respected by her nor loved. He bores
her—and with her, boredom and hatred are
near neighbours.

Ideal Marriage, p, 49.

"ANY MAIL FOR me?" I asked, as soon as I arrived home
from the trip.

"I don't *recall* any," said my father, as if searching his
memory. But later, when everyone was seated at dinner, he
went into the kitchen and brought out a letter from Jessica on a
silver platter, garnished with parsley.

"I thought so," I said, feeling my spirits soar. Seeing
Jessica's handwriting on the envelope, with her familiar flourishes, I was swept again with love for her. I put the letter into
my pocket.

"Aren't you going to share your *billet-doux* with us?" my
father asked.

"I think I'll wait," I said, wanting to save the letter until
later and enjoy looking forward to reading it.

When I got into bed, I opened the letter:

> Dear Andre,
> There is something I need to tell
> you. Ironically, after all the bad things I

said about him, my old boyfriend Michael and I have been seeing each other again. I know I should have told you earlier, but I didn't want to hurt you, especially right before your class trip. You are one of the nicest boys—one of the nicest people of either sex—that I've ever known. That's what makes this so difficult for me.

I might be making a terrible mistake. Part of me thinks so, that I'm throwing away something that could be really good. But another part of me doesn't, and I have to listen to that part, too. This probably sounds awful, but I feel comfortable with Michael. We know each other's good points and bad points and I want to see where things go between us.

Maybe I feel too young and scared to get involved in something so deep as I know it would be between you and me. And since we live in different cities, a relationship couldn't just develop naturally between us. You know, like a study date on a weekday, or a Coke after school.

Andre, I want so much for us to stay good friends. Not just like people say "good friends" without meaning it, but really good friends. Believe me, you are very important to me. But under the circumstances, I think it would be fairest toward everyone if we cancel our date for my prom.

I hope you can find it in your heart to forgive this silly girl for writing you this letter that she so much hates to have to do. If anyone deserves to be happy, it's certainly you. I know that someday you'll find a

girl with the maturity to treasure and
respond to the fine person that you are.
Your friend for as long as you want
me to be,

Jessica Dane.

I turned over in bed, face down. Pressing my mouth against
the pillow so no one would hear me, I yelled, "No! No! Please,
let it be just a dream." Recalling my mother's warning against
lying face down—"You could smother in your sleep"—I turned
onto my back. Then I got up and put on my record of
Beethoven's Ninth, the side containing the final movement.

Listening to it only made me sadder. Without Jessica's love,
even Beethoven's music seemed meaningless. The soloists'
singing out, "*Freude*," which previously had always moved me,
now seemed a mockery. Tonight was the lowest point in my
life.

I awoke the next morning, surprised at having fallen asleep
at all. At school I took in little of what anyone said, my mind
continuously on Jessica.

On my way home I walked over subway and cellar gratings.
While I'd never intentionally commit suicide, I thought that, if
anyone was to die from a loose grating, it should be me, who
had less to live for than other people. At least I could serve as a
voluntary grating inspector.

In the evening, I listened to Hank Thompson singing, "My
tears have washed 'I love you' from the blackboard of my
heart," and Hank Williams singing, "Some day you'll call my
name and I won't answer." Then I felt almost cheerful, until I
awoke the next morning and missed Jessica again.

When we were in the Museum of Modern Art, she had told
me how lucky she felt to be standing in front of Munch's painting, *The Silent Scream*, instead of feeling whatever was making
the man scream. So why was Jessica doing it to *me* now, turning me into the screamer, filled with despair?

While riding on buses, I looked at extremely old women.
Then I imagined Jessica, too, shriveling into little more than

95

wrinkled skin stretched over a skull and bones. The image warmed me till the end of the ride.

Walking in Central Park, I ignored the statue of Alice in Wonderland and went over to The Ugly Duckling instead. I touched Hans Christian Anderson's shoulder and said to him, sadly, "I guess we share the same fate now."

I missed Jessica most on first awakening each morning. With tears in my eyes, I thought how senseless it was that she and I were living at the same time, even in the same country, and yet were apart. Her letter to me had even admitted that she might be making a terrible mistake, "throwing away something that could be really good."

Jessica *was* making a terrible mistake, I thought. She was destroying something that could have been wonderful. I hadn't been wrong about her. She had shown in her letter that she, too, had felt that we had something good between us. How could I make her see that all we needed was the courage to try?

I vowed never to become cynical about love. I'd rather risk being hurt repeatedly, I thought through my tears, than stop daring to love.

Ideal Marriage said that the best means of defense against marital ennui, outside the sexual sphere, was "a strong mutual interest in some subject."

I wrote a letter to Jessica, emphasizing our common interests. Since she had previously complained that her boyfriend Michael disliked museums, I described the Frick Museum in detail, including its plush chairs and beautiful interior pond, around which I was seated while writing to her. I also mentioned having gone to a concert and walked through the peaceful courtyards of the Cloisters—interests I thought Michael unlikely to share, although (I admitted to myself) I had mainly enjoyed imagining describing them to Jessica.

"I hope you will have a very happy life," I ended my letter to her. "Since I love you, I wish you all the best, whatever choices you make." Surely, that sounded mature, I thought.

I added a "P.S.":

Jessica, one thing troubles me, for *your* sake: that your body contains certain secrets to realizing its full capacity for delight. I had planned to reveal them to you in the future when you were ready. Now I only hope that Michael knows them, too, and how to unlock them for you. They are subtle, but wondrous, with the potential to make you quiver with pleasure. While I'd hate for you to miss out on them, under the circumstances I think it would be indiscreet of me now to go into details.

I knew I had no idea what I was talking about, but I hoped it would intrigue Jessica and make her wonder what she was missing out on. If she ever came back to me and asked for specifics, I would find some in *Ideal Marriage*, such as that erotic sensitivity increased from the periphery of the body toward the center. I pictured Michael caressing Jessica in the wrong direction—from the center, toward the periphery—diminishing her desire until it disappeared.

I also stopped reading both *Ideal Marriage* and *Economics*. Now that Jessica had broken off with me, they kept reminding me that I'd been reading them to prepare for our no-longer-existing future together.

During this low point in my life, my sister, Alice, came through for me, making up for all our past fights. She invited me to hang out with her and her girlfriends, and I gratefully accepted.

"I want to be there for you," she said to me. "I hope you know by now that I'm a good person."

"I do," I said, suppressing my dislike for Alice's "I'm-a-good-person" line, although in this case it was true.

I joined Alice and her friends for movies and sodas and discussions of the "weird boys" in her class. I even became something of a hero to her friends. Alice told them that I was a "star-crossed lover," because my sweetheart wouldn't wait for me until we were old enough to get married. They called me romantic and swore that, if *they* were in love with someone like me, they would wait for him until they could get married, however long it took.

"Be sincere," declared the advice columns in Alice's teenage magazines. "Any boy who won't accept you for who you are doesn't deserve your love. Be glad you're rid of him."

It was awful advice, I thought. If anything, I'd been *too* sincere with Jessica. I had told her too soon that I loved her. Like Brian suggested, I should have played it cooler.

I felt embarrassed to tell either Brian or Pam about Jessica's having broken off with me, after I'd talked about her so much. It was Pam who finally brought it up.

"What's wrong, Andre?" she said to me after school one day. "The cherry blossoms are out, the magnolias are blooming in the park, but you look miserable. Come along."

Pam took my hand and led me into Central Park, where we sat down on a patch of grass away from anyone else.

"Jessica broke up with me," I blurted out.

"I thought so." Pam reached over and hugged me. "Poor Andre. You must feel terrible. Remember that we love you, that Brian and I both love you."

"Thanks," I said. "I love you both, too." I felt tears coming, tears of thankfulness for their love, I thought.

"Andre, you're a very sensitive boy," said Pam, hugging me again. "It's a wonderful quality. But maybe you're *too* sensitive, too nice to people.

"I'm going to tell you a secret. Girls don't want a nice guy, not the kind of boy their mother wants them to date. They want an outlaw. But an outlaw who they alone can tame. Maybe you should become more of an outlaw, Andre."

That could be the key, I thought. I felt myself reaching for it. It was what Brian had said about making girls serve him, instead of the other way around. I pictured myself like Jack Palance in *Shane*, completely calm and dripping with evil. I snapped my fingers, as if dropping a girl who proved unworthy of my love. On leaving the park, I assumed just the hint of a swagger, so my outlaw look wouldn't seem exaggerated.

Over the summer I worked for a grain company owned by a friend of my father's in Kansas City. I was stationed at one of the company's grain elevators in Altus, Oklahoma, where the temperature often exceeded 100 degrees. The sun and heat reflected off the aluminum silo roofs and seemed to head straight for me.

When farmers drove in with a load of wheat, I climbed up onto their truck to weigh the wheat and test it for moisture. I reached my sampling dipper down into the wheat as far as my arm extended, having been warned that the farmers would pile their dry grain on top to conceal the wet stuff underneath.

I usually ate dinner at a diner that served cheap steaks and homemade chocolate pie. Then I'd go back to my motel room and read, hardly cooling myself with the fan, the motel having no air-conditioning.

On some evenings, I went to the town's one movie theater, even if I'd already seen the film. At least, the theater had air-conditioning, and twice the tornado whistle sounded, lending excitement, as we all scattered to a shelter in the basement.

On other evenings, I joined some of the local teenage boys in their nightly entertainment—cruising around the central square, searching for carloads of girls to talk with, then driving out to the edge of town to "look at the cloud" and try to predict whether a tornado was approaching.

On one particularly hot night, I lay awake in bed, as usual missing Jessica. I tried to imagine her gradually maturing to the point where she'd no longer be scared of a deep involvement with me, as she'd said in her letter. Then I found myself thinking about one of the local boys, who had mentioned having "made it" with chickens.

The idea seemed disgusting. I recalled the chicken coops I'd seen, full of dry, weedy grasses and pellets of corn and excrement. Would I even fit inside a chicken? I wondered. Probably yes, I figured, since eggs came out of chickens, even "jumbo" eggs. But what if the chicken flapped around and pecked me while my pants were down, or a rooster or other chickens came over and pecked me while I was inside the first chicken?

Of course, there were more reasonable animals—a sheep that had been cleaned off by a heavy rain, like the pure, white sheep on Jessica's nightgown, or a large, peaceful dog that had recently been given a bath, like a golden retriever or an Irish setter. I could more easily imagine being turned on by a sheep or a dog than a chicken.

Perhaps I could learn about sex through first doing it with an animal? I would practice matching my rhythm to that of the sheep or dog, waiting to come until she was ready, too. Then I'd apply what I had learned to a woman, provided she and the animal had similar rhythms.

But supposing a sheep went into a vaginal spasm with me inside it? I would feel humiliated walking into a hospital emergency room stuck inside a sheep, or even a dog. Or what if I reached orgasm before the animal did? I pictured a ewe or an Irish Setter, turning around and looking at me disappointedly after I had finished too soon and gone limp.

"Every college is a good college, if you make it so," the guidance counselor told our new senior class when school reopened in September. Then he privately advised certain students to apply to the "good colleges," a group I fortunately fell into, having been getting more "A's" than "B's."

My own criteria for colleges included good academics, a high ratio of girls to boys, and a reasonable climate. I ruled out Yale and Princeton for being all male; Chicago and Kenyon for their cold winters; and Dartmouth for both reasons.

I applied to Harvard and Swarthmore, along with Cornell,

in spite of its cold winters and three-to-one ratio of boys to girls. While both Harvard and Swarthmore had fine academic reputations, Swarthmore offered a better climate, a higher ratio of teachers to students, and an equal number of girls and boys. And since Swarthmore had been founded by the Friends, my having a Quaker mother might help me get admitted.

I also took a battery of vocational guidance tests, looking for advice on a future career. But three hours of testing revealed only that I was "unlikely to become a religious leader." Nonetheless, I found myself chosen as the object of religious love at school that semester.

Although politically leftist, Mattoon had a small but fervent Christian Association, known as the "CA." The majority of its members were fundamentalists, and Bob Bradshaw, the most militant of them and a fellow senior, lived only five blocks away from me.

He appeared at our home one Sunday morning in September. I had been sitting in the living room with my parents, listening to Gilbert and Sullivan on the radio.

Bradshaw was wearing tan slacks and a red viyella shirt. He was tall and chubby, with rosy cheeks, a clean-shaven face, and neatly-combed, wetted brown hair. I remembered him with a scruffy beard the previous semester. He and I had occasionally played ping pong on a table in Mattoon's basement, with me winning most of the games.

"May I take up a few minutes of your time?" Bradshaw asked me now.

"Sure," I said, surprised at his formality. After introducing him to my parents, I led him into my room.

"Hi!" said Bradshaw. He reached out to shake hands and then smiled. "That handshake was a test. When I held out my hand to you and you shook it, you signaled your readiness to open your heart to God. These little tests are important, you know. Like, my name is Robert, but I tell people, 'Call me Bob.' It shows everyone what kind of person I am.

"I have come today on a *joyful* mission," he continued. "I'm here to tell you that the Christian Association has voted

101

you our 'Focus Of Love' this year." He beamed at me. "We sense that your heart is unfulfilled, and we want to invite you to come to our next meeting and receive the Good News."

I hesitated, then agreed. While neither Christian nor religious, I liked the idea of being someone's "focus of love," even the CA's.

Bradshaw told me that, before his rebirth, he had lived as a sinner—drinking, playing poker, "fornicating" with his girlfriend. "But that life is all over for me. I'm not the same Bob Bradshaw anymore. If Christ could reach down low enough to save a miserable sinner like me, I tell you there's hope for everyone. He loves each of us, no matter what we've done or how we've sinned."

As Bradshaw went on about his rebirth, I found myself more interested in his former life as a sinner.

"Bob, I'm delighted that you're filled with Christ's love," I said. "But do you ever miss your previous life a little, like sleeping with your girlfriend?"

"Yeah, I think about it sometimes." Bradshaw sighed. "But then I tell myself, 'Hey, Bob, remember, only our Lord Christ was perfect.' Bradshaw flipped through his pocket New Testament, with protruding bookmarks. "'If we say that we have no sin, we deceive ourselves,'" he read aloud from John's First Epistle. "Now here's the glorious part: 'He cleanseth us from all sin.'"

"That's wonderful," I said. "I'm happy for you.... Bob, *before* you were reborn, what kind of birth control did you use?"

"Rita had a diaphragm. She hated the cheap rubbers I bought—the twenty-five cent, no-lube jobs." Bradshaw shook his head.

"It shows you how low I'd fallen, before I nailed my sins to the Cross and asked Christ's forgiveness. That's what I want to talk with you about, Christ's infinite forgiveness."

"I'd love to hear about it. Just one more question, first. Did you prefer using a diaphragm? Was it better than even a *good* rubber?"

"Yeah, the diaphragm." Bradshaw grinned. "I mean, what the hell, Rita was the one using it. Excuse my language—it's something I still have to work on."

The CA held their weekday meetings in an empty school-room and their Sunday meetings at a member's home.

"Dear Lord," intoned their president, Ted McCabe, at their next meeting, "we ask you to welcome and to bless Andre Schulman." McCabe lifted up his arms. Today, Andre has taken his first step toward reserving a place by Thy side. Once he is reborn in Thy Son, his reservation will be confirmed."

Several CA members touched my arm and smiled at me as if I'd already converted. I resisted an impulse to announce my conversion on the spot and make everyone happy.

Preben Anderson, one of the CA's better students, argued that believers had an edge over non-believers. "If the atheists are right," he said, "then we're all in the same boat after death. We're nothing. But if *we're* right, we go up and they go down. So aren't you better off believing? You lose nothing, and you may gain everything."

I liked the argument, the idea of a possible gain with no risk of loss. But was my hoping that something was true—that God existed, or that Jessica would come back to me, I thought sadly—reason enough to believe in it?

A pre-requisite to becoming a member of the CA was to have experienced rebirth in Christ. I learned that, a few months after he'd become a member, Bradshaw had announced that he'd undergone a second, more profound rebirth and that he now thought he might have only imagined the first, out of a desire to join. Ever since, he was known in the CA as "Born Again Again Bradshaw."

Before traveling anywhere, the CA members gathered to pray for a safe trip. On returning, they met a second time to give thanks for a safe return. I envied how those rituals of prayer and thanksgiving enhanced their lives, turning everyday events into causes for celebration.

My own Thanksgiving that year felt dead to me, without sharing it with Jessica. I had secretly hoped that, as Thanksgiving approached, she would decide that she wanted to spend it with me again.

My parents had invited my father's parents and an unmarried teacher friend of my mother's. Her own parents were celebrating Thanksgiving with their other two children, my uncles.

When everyone's plate had been filled, my father tapped on his water glass with a spoon, for silence.

"It is only fitting today," he said, "that we should offer our thanks to the country that we are all so fortunate to be living in. The only democracy powerful enough to resist Communist aggression. The one hope for the survival of the free world as we know it." He lifted his wine glass. "To the United States of America, our country right, or wrong."

"How about a toast to peace?" said my mother. "It's something we can all agree on."

"Karen, don't be so weak-kneed!" said my father. "That's the way of appeasement. Again, I propose to you, 'Our country, right or wrong.'"

"Wait, Dad," I said, "you've left something out." Why was I speaking? I wondered. "The full saying is, 'Our country, right or wrong. When right, to be kept right; when wrong, to be put right.'"

"Another county heard from," said my father. "But thank you, I've learned something. However, while you may be right technically, and I assume that you are, I put it to you that your emphasis is misplaced. There is a more important issue at stake here—our willingness to stand up for our country and show a little gratitude to it."

"I still think 'peace' is the best toast," said my mother.

"I'm saying nothing," said my grandmother. "I have my own opinion, but I'm not foolish enough to come between my son and my daughter-in-law."

"All right," said my father, shaking his head. "Everyone drink to his own sentiments and we'll leave it at that. But I think it's shameful we couldn't do better. You're making a travesty out of Thanksgiving."

No one spoke for a while. As at Quaker Meetings, I wondered who would break the silence.

Eventually, my father did. "It would be untenable," he said, "for New York State not to stand behind its moral obligation bonds. Even if the state has no *legal* obligation to make good on them, the public thinks of them as 'full faith and credit' bonds."

While my father spoke about bonds and then the "gloomy prospects" for the Middle East, I recalled the previous Thanksgiving at Jessica's, with her house full of cheer and laughter.

I finally made the basketball team, as a senior. I was tenth man on an eleven-man squad. For most of the season, I got into games only after they were no longer in doubt, and I scored a total of zero points. Yet, I never missed a practice session.

Four days a week, for an hour and a half after school, I practiced shooting and guarding, passing and setting picks, trying to make up in zeal for what I lacked in talent. The coach praised my hustle when I stole passes in scrimmages against the starting team, and he held me up as a model to the better but lazier players.

"Andre plays his heart out, while the rest of you jokers goof off," he reprimanded them. "I'm warning everyone, if you don't get off your cans, no one's position is secure."

Reveling in the coach's praise, I felt basketball practice bringing me back to life. My ache at having lost Jessica began to recede. After each practice session I felt pleasantly tired, and I slept well at night again and could concentrate on studying.

"Always keep working on your peripheral vision," the coach kept exhorting the team. I took every opportunity to do so. When crossing streets, I looked straight ahead, trying to judge oncoming traffic without turning toward it. When talking with someone, I averted my head almost 45 degrees and still tried to read the person's face. I imagined myself a peripheral-vision specialist, put into the game to steal passes until the other team caught on.

Above all, I took pride in being part of the team and wearing the Mattoon uniform—the pale-green shirt and shorts, the glossy bright-green warm-up jacket, with my number, 7, in tan chenille. I was glad that the numbers were assigned arbitrarily, rather than reflecting my standing on the team. At pre-game warm-ups, I was issued a stick of Juicy Fruit gum, just like the players who mattered, and I got to join in the team's strategy huddles with the coach and the laying-on of hands and yelling, "Go!" before each half started.

Still, I felt sad at times, seeing other girls wearing their boyfriends' warm-up jackets and knowing that Jessica would never wear mine.

I also sensed I was an impostor, like Uncle Marvel in the *Marvel Family* comics. While Captain Marvel, Mary Marvel, and Captain Marvel Junior all had super-human strength and could fly, Uncle Marvel only *believed* he had those powers. The other Marvels covered up for him when fighting criminals and supported him while flying without his realizing it. Like Uncle Marvel, I thought, I, too, was wearing the team uniform without contributing to its victories.

In Mattoon's final game, in mid-February, we were leading Central Needle Trades High by eight points, with only four minutes left, when one of our starting guards fouled out. Then his replacement slipped on a spot where the Needle Trades center had dripped perspiration.

"Andre, go in and play defense," the coach said to me.

For the first time, I was entering a game that was still in doubt.

As the two Needle Trades guards brought up the ball, I hung back in my zone, to prevent anyone's cutting around me. Out of the corner of my eye, I saw one of the guards pass the ball cross-court. I shot forward and batted the ball away. Then I picked it up and dribbled toward the Needle Trades' basket. No one was blocking my way. Feeling myself growing panicky, I called up my dream of making love with the girl in the green

106

dress. I kept picturing the dream as I laid the ball up off the backboard and into the basket.

Then I scurried back down the court to get ready on defense again. But Needle Trades called "time out," and our coach took me out of the game and put back in the guard I had replaced, whose ankle was now taped.

"You did good," the coach said to me. "And you made them use up their final 'time out.'"

"Way to go, Andre!" someone yelled from the stands.

I felt wonderful. Sitting on the bench, I let the realization wash over me. I had scored in a game and when it counted. My two points would appear in the Mattoon record book, wiping out the zero next to my name. Then I put off further thought about it and cheered Mattoon on to victory through the final three minutes of the game.

On our way to the soda fountain afterward, Brian congratulated me on my basket.

I felt prouder than ever of wearing my Mattoon jacket. No longer was I an Uncle Marvel, participating only second-hand in the team's exploits. I ordered two nickel Cokes—a cherry and a chocolate Coke—convinced I got more that way than from one dime Coke, and I sipped the Cokes alternately, going from flavor to flavor. It was the finest day of my life.

What my dream of making love had been trying to teach me, I realized now, was not about technique, but serenity. Surely I was maturing.

I returned to the Museum of Modern Art, in spite of my fear of its re-awakening my sadness over Jessica.

But this time I walked in the opposite direction of the crowd, to see more women. I realized that I would rather look at a live, attractive woman than at almost any painting. Even a beautiful Renoir nude, her breasts dappled in light, interested me less than two girls I saw standing in front of it. With other artists, the contrast was still greater. If Fernand Léger wanted to paint people to resemble factory pipes, expressing the inhumanity of the Industrial Age, that was his right. But once I'd gotten Leger's point, why go on looking at his tubular women? And while I admired the industriousness of the pointillists, I questioned their painting thousands of colored dots simply to reveal a sailboat. Was it worth all that effort for so little payoff?

While flipping through one of my mother's *Vogue* magazines at home, I came upon an ad titled, "Subtly provocative in black silk marquisette and a point-of-view décolletage etched in palest pink satin." The ad showed a woman in a dress with a lacy top, intimating bare breasts and skin underneath. The term "point-of-view décolletage" seemed to heighten the excitement, implying that I could make out the woman's bare body if only I looked carefully enough. Now *that* was a better use of pointillism, I thought. It gave me a lot more for my trouble than just seeing a sailboat.

I also picked up *Economics* and *Ideal Marriage* again. Although I still missed Jessica, I was determined to go on preparing for my future, even if it had to be without her.

In *Economics* I plunged into Keynes' challenge to classical economics and its view that the economy would always tend towards full employment—by wages and interest rates' adjusting until it was reached.

Now here was Keynes, showing that equilibrium could exist along with unemployment—that in bad times, even if workers were willing to accept a lower wage, they might remain unemployed. Their lower wages would leave them with less purchasing power, which, in turn, would lead to lower production, further reducing the demand for labor. Wages, production, and employment would all spiral downward.

Keynes's theory excited me, with its equations and intersecting curves, and its "consumption function" and "multiplier effect," even if I didn't yet know how I could make use of them.

It reminded me of the time that our math teacher, Mrs. Nichtinhauser, a German refugee, had been explaining ratios in class, and Franklin Dubois had asked her, "Could you give us an example of a ratio?"

"*Nein!*" Mrs. Nichtinhauser had exploded. "I'm not teaching apples and oranges. I am teaching the beauty of the ratio itself."

What a wonderful idea, I thought, the beauty of the ratio itself.

In *Ideal Marriage*, I read that the erotic kiss "is rich in variations. It may 'brush the bloom' like a butterfly's wing by a light stroking of lips with other pursed lips.

> From its lightest, faintest form, it may run the gamut of intimacy and intensity to the pitch of *Maraichinage*, in which the couple, sometimes for hours, mutually explore and caress the inside of each other's mouths with their tongues, as profoundly as possible.
>
> The *tongue* is indispensable in the erotic kiss; and 'plays lead' in its most important variations. The tongue-kiss is most captivating when the tip of the tongue very lightly and gently titillates the beloved's tongue and lips.

I wished that I had read those passages before visiting Jessica over Thanksgiving. When her tongue had touched mine, I would have responded in kind, with all the subtlety and variety described in *Ideal Marriage*. Maybe then she wouldn't have broken off with me.

The CA's campaign to convert me grew in intensity. Barely a day went by without Bradshaw's asking if I had heard the "clear, sweet voice" inside myself yet, or a CA member's reminding me, as I left the school lunchroom, "Bible study in ten minutes."

Yet, I found my mind wandering during CA meetings. While the others argued over whether playing rock music was allowable if you substituted religious words for the dirty lyrics, I pondered Trappist jellies. I wondered whether the Trappists' vow of silence prevented them from pointing out any defects in their jellies before they got to market. Just to be safe, I thought we should buy other brands.

I felt grateful to the CA for the refuge they had offered me when I'd been so down. It had taken my mind off the constant ache of missing Jessica, even if only temporarily. But now I felt stronger and that I no longer needed that refuge. At the CA's next Sunday-morning gathering at Bradshaw's, I told them that I knew I wasn't going to convert.

"I'm sorry," I said. "I really appreciate all the time and effort you've put in with me. It's meant a lot to me, more than I can tell you. The way all of you reached out to me when you saw I was in need."

Ted McCabe, their president, came over and put an arm around me. "Of course, we're disappointed," he said. "But for *you*, not for *us*." The others nodded agreement and said they hoped I would change my mind in the future.

Only Bradshaw wouldn't give up.

"May I talk about it with you?" he asked, following me to the door.

"Sure," I said, "if you want to walk along with me. But I have to walk fast." I looked at my watch and headed out briskly. "We're having breakfast in eighteen minutes." Sunday morning was pancakes or waffles, and I didn't want to miss them.

"You may not believe this," said Bradshaw, hurrying alongside me, "but I'm glad you're making it tough on me. I know that it's God's way of testing me. Andre, I beg of you, even if you don't care about yourself, think of your immortal soul."

I sensed an idea forming. "Bob," I said, "you say that you know God's testing you with me. I have a suggestion. Let's play a game of ping pong for my soul. If you win, I'll keep going to the CA meetings until graduation. But if *I* win, you and the CA call off your campaign."

"I can't do it," said Bradshaw. "Christ doesn't let us put tests to Him."

"You're *not* putting a test to him. As you yourself said, it's a test that *he's* putting to *you*. Think about it—if God really

110

wants me to convert, he will strengthen your arm and you'll beat me. Bob, this may be the one chance he's giving you. Don't blow it."

Bradshaw finally agreed, and we settled on a two-out-of-three match the following day, on the school ping pong table.

I eked out the first game, 21-18, favoring my backhand, because my forehand and slam felt tight.

Bradshaw easily won the next game, 21-10, hitting to my forehand and waiting for setups and smashing them. Near the end of the game, when I was down 19-7, I tried a few slams, figuring I'd nothing to lose. I won the next three points, lifting my confidence, but then lost the final two.

As we changed ends between games, I sent up a silent prayer. "God, if you let me win, I promise I'll go back to Quaker meetings and I'll keep an open mind."

I jumped out to a six-nothing lead, fearlessly using both my forehand and backhand. Then my touch deserted me again. After missing two slams, I became overcautious, letting Bradshaw take the offensive. He gradually caught up until I was leading by only 16 to 14. On the next point, I noticed him cheating.

At first, I wasn't sure. I hit a deep shot that nicked the end of the table, but Bradshaw called it out.

"I heard it touch," I said.

Bradshaw shook his head. "I saw it out."

Three shots later, he called the score 17-16, when I knew it was 18-16. Unable to agree, we played the last point over, which Bradshaw won. Then at 19-19, I returned his serve with a cut, winning the point. But Bradshaw called his own serve a "let."

"No, it was *way* above the net," I said. "If you're really reborn, how come you're cheating?" I felt carried along by my own outburst. "For *your* sake, Bob, you should ask God's forgiveness. Think of your immortal soul."

"I, I, I'm sorry," Bradshaw stammered. His face reddened. "I, I did it for Christ. I felt that He wanted me to win."

"I understand, Bob. But tell me honestly, on how many

111

points did you cheat? Remember the Bible—'Thou shalt not tell a lie.'"

"It was only the last point," said Bradshaw.... "Well, maybe one other."

"Okay," I said. "Let's assume you're right—that those were the only two points. Then I win, 21-18. My 19, plus the two points you cheated on. Good match!"

I hurried over to shake Bradshaw's hand before he realized the consequence of his admission.

"You played well," I said. "It could've gone either way."

Chapter Eight

A POOR THOREAU

> If *erotic genius* does not charac-
> terise him, the man needs *explicit knowl-*
> *edge* .... He must *know how to make love.*
> *Ideal Marriage*, p. 9.

I WENT TO Friends Meeting the following Sunday, keeping my promise that, if I beat Bradshaw at ping pong, I would return to Quaker Meetings with an open mind.

The two-story-high Meeting house, on Rutherford Place, was made of red brick with white window frames. The Meeting room itself had tall windows, a few ceiling lamps, and rows of plain benches on three sides of the room.

The Meeting began with some fifteen minutes of silence, a period the Quakers called "centering down." Then a thin, seventyish woman in a pink sweater stood up to speak.

"I was in my kitchen this morning, doing the breakfast dishes," she said. "Suddenly, a ray of sunlight hit my dishwater and made tiny rainbows in the soap bubbles. 'How beautiful is nature,' I thought. 'It finds a way to visit me even when I'm doing my dishes.'"

I felt like applauding. After months of CA meetings, I found the woman's story of rainbows in her soap bubbles refreshing.

Another ten minutes or so of silence followed. Then a thin man in gray trousers and a gray sweater stood up. Most of the Quakers seemed to run thin, I'd noticed.

"You may have observed that I'm dressed in gray," said the man. "It's because we Quakers see the world as neither all white nor all black. I wanted to share that thought with you and to say that I'm still meditating on last week's message about frogs in a pail of milk. For me it was a deeply spiritual message."

I tried to picture a few frogs swimming around in a pail of milk. What were the frogs doing in the milk, I wondered, and what was their "message"? It might have been the most interesting message of the year and I'd missed it.

Near the end of the Meeting, two men rose together and for several minutes chanted, "Krishna, Krishna; Hari, Hari." Chanting Krishna's name was "the only path to true enlightenment," said one of the men.

After they sat down and the obligatory five minutes for contemplating the message had passed, a woman stood up and said merely, "Quaker silences are the deepest form of communication."

During the post-Meeting coffee hour, one of the "elders" came over to welcome me.

"The Society of Friends considers *all* speech a ministry," he said. "But sometimes it can be a very trying ministry. As soon as some members stand up in Meeting, you cringe. You know they're going to go on and on. When that happens, several longtime Friends might stand up in silent reproach. We call it 'eldering.'"

In between Meetings, I tried to emulate the Quakers in looking for beauty all around me. Walking over subway gratings, I savored the warm air blowing up from them in winter, as I had enjoyed the cool air they gave off in summer. Trudging through Central Park, I observed the formica glistening in rocks, the veins on fallen, dead leaves, and the brown and tan splotches on the Turkey oaks, looking like giraffes.

Strolling around the rowboat lake, I admired the ducks gliding under the romantic Bow Bridge. But I wished that a beautiful woman were perched on one of the off-shore rocks, like the diaphanously-clad girl in the "White Rock" ad.

I would have made a poor Thoreau, I thought. Given a choice between girls and nature, nature would lose every time. Seeing couples in bright, winter coats and scarves, their arms wrapped around each other and a free hand holding a cup of hot chocolate or coffee, I knew I would trade in a whole forest of trees to be part of such a couple. However beautiful nature might be, it could never make up for Jessica.

"My love," I addressed her, "you are infinitely more precious to me than the liveliest squirrel or the subtlest leaf pattern."

I vowed to keep my love for her alive until she felt ready to accept it. In the meantime my love would have to be strong enough for both of us.

At the next Meeting, nobody spoke during the entire hour. I cherished even the slightest diversion—people crossing or uncrossing their legs, or coughing. The coughs seemed to go across the room, like the sections of an orchestra coming in on cue. I kept shifting my angle of vision, trying to make as many heads as possible overlap any single head. My maximum was five.

I eventually settled my eyes on a plump girl with a sweet face and the middle button of her blouse undone.

Was everyone but me thinking spiritual thoughts? I wondered. Many at Meeting were sitting with their heads bowed. I bowed mine, too, and tried to be spiritual. But I found myself making a wish.

"Please, let me lose my virginity," I silently entreated the Quaker Spirit. I hoped that the Spirit was broadminded enough to accept my desires without judging them.

Raising my head again, I noticed a tall blonde with luxuriant hair. It flowed down over her shoulders and the black sweater she was wearing with a pearl necklace. Her hair glowed, luminous in a shaft of sunlight that must have entered through a break in the clouds.

"Let others seek beauty in nature," I thought. I preferred

beauty in women. Maybe I'd speak up in Meeting and share that message. I wondered whether the blonde slept without a pajama top, as I did. I imagined us lying together, chest to chest, with only our bottoms on.

Unlike my father, I always slept with my pajama bottoms on. It seemed more decent. One evening I had been reading on the easy chair in my parents' bedroom while my mother lay on her bed in a nightgown, and my father played solitaire on his own bed in a dressing gown. Suddenly, I noticed my father's penis emerging from the folds of his dressing gown, like a dog's penis appearing from within its fur.

"Ernest, you're being obscene," my mother said to him. It confirmed my decision to go on wearing my bottoms.

The silence in the Meeting House eventually stopped bothering me. I felt myself relaxing, centering down at last. I thought of Jessica again, but peacefully now.

I thanked her silently for setting a standard for me. I wouldn't marry anyone lesser.

I also realized another thing. Before Jessica broke off with me, I had made every day and night magical through continually envisioning her beside me. Whenever I was out walking, I imagined us holding hands. When waiting for a green light at street corners, instead of fidgeting impatiently like my father, Jessica and I would kiss, welcoming the delay. But ever since the break-up, my days had become ordinary again, no longer enhanced by her "presence." In breaking off with me, she had deprived me of not only her love, but also the delight of picturing us together.

There were two possibilities—either she would come back to me someday, or she wouldn't. Then why not assume that she *would* come back and let myself once again enjoy her imagined presence, especially at night? I had nothing to lose, so long as I acted in the real world on the assumption that she wouldn't come back.

I thought again about the Christian Association. Previously, I had felt patronizing toward them, thinking them naive for believing Christ was ever present in their lives. But now I reconsidered. Hadn't I and the CA members been doing the same thing—heightening our lives through imagining the presence of a being that was physically absent? And hadn't our lives been enriched by such imaginings, whether or not they corresponded with external reality?

After the Meeting, I picked up a pamphlet from a rack in the entranceway. The pamphlet stated that, while anyone might speak at Meeting, "the weightier Friends tend to sit near the front and to speak more often."

I continued to consider speaking up at Meeting about the beauty of women. Thinking that the Quakers had been over-praising nature, I wanted to restore a sense of balance. But instead of planning a speech in advance, I would await inspiration's tap.

In the middle of the next Meeting, I suddenly stood up, then immediately felt dizzy. I realized I had gone beyond the point of no return. I could no longer just sit back down again and blend into the crowd.

"I was sitting here in Meeting last week," I began. "I was thinking ... I was thinking that springtime is almost in the air." (I spoke haltingly, to convey sincerity.) "Then I saw a ray of sunshine touch the face of a beautiful young woman and ... and light up her hair. Nature was using the sun's rays to reveal human beauty.

"In that moment, the inner Spirit revealed something to me. That we don't have to look for beauty just *outside* in nature. It's right here in our own Meetinghouse. Not only in that beautiful woman lit up by nature's sunlight, but in everyone here at Meeting ... each beautiful in his or her own way." Then I sat down, aware that I'd added the last phrase to be diplomatic.

I feared that I'd made a fool of myself. But I believed in what I had said.

No one mentioned my "message" when I arrived at the post-Meeting, coffee hour.

"Isn't it a glorious day out?" said the elder who had previously spoken about cringing whenever certain Friends got up to speak.

"Yes," I replied, "it's my favorite time of year." I felt relieved that he was still talking to me. "You notice the days getting longer, but all of spring and summer are still ahead."

"I find that nature has her secrets to reveal in *every* season," said the elder. Then he moved off, leaving me to wonder whether I'd just received a Quaker reprimand.

I began to wish that someone would at least *mention* my message, would consider it worth commenting on.

Finally, while drifting towards the cookie table, I heard a voice say, "Thank you for your message today. I found it challenging." I recognized the man in gray who had announced that he was still meditating on the frogs in a pail of milk.

A girl came up beside me as I was leaving the Meeting house the following Sunday.

"Pardon me," she said. "I don't want to disturb you—"

"You're *not*." She was the girl who had been sitting at an earlier Meeting with a middle button of her blouse undone.

"I wanted to tell you that I admired your ministry last week," she said. "It took a lot of courage."

"Thanks," I said, once I realized what she was talking about. "But I just said what I thought."

"I know. I could tell you were being sincere."

"I was planning to go out for an egg cream," I said. "May I invite you to join me? Incidentally, I'm Andre Schulman." It seemed only polite to introduce myself.

"Pleased to meet you, Andre Schulman." She reached out a white-gloved hand. "I'm Doris Turnbull. And I'd love to have an egg cream."

We walked to a soda fountain on Third Avenue and sat down at a booth. I felt torn between a vanilla and a chocolate egg cream. The vanilla could be subtler, I knew, but it could also taste like little more than weakly-flavored seltzer. Chocolate egg creams were more dependable, if potentially less interesting. I ordered chocolate, Doris vanilla.

She looked sweet, I thought, even if a little plump. She had dark hair and a round face and was dressed neatly in a navy blue jacket, light-blue skirt, and a buttoned-up, white blouse. Except for not wearing a hat, she looked like someone I would expect more to see coming from church than from Meeting.

"I like your outfit," I said, reaching for a term that wouldn't betray my ignorance of fashion.

"Well, thank you. I do like to dress up for Meeting." Doris smiled as if she'd confided a secret.

She said that she was a sophomore at NYU, majoring in English and minoring in music.

"I'm sorry, I'm just a high-school senior," I said, feeling diminished. I had thought Doris was younger.

"Don't apologize. You seem more mature than most college guys I know. They think it's so cool to act blasé about everything."

I felt better at her calling me "mature."

"Do you have any roommates?" I asked, to make conversation.

"Only Kita, my tan labrador." Doris said that she lived alone in a studio on West 4th Street, near NYU, so she could cook and keep her dog. At the college cafeteria, everything sat around on steam trays, losing all taste, or was greasy with meat fat. She said that she preferred to have fresh vegetables that she cooked for herself.

"Now you know my weird side."

"Well, I have my own weird side," I said. "Like I won't eat strawberry ice cream, with all those little bits of strawberry in it. Doris, from one weird person to another, would you like to go out next Saturday, if you're free?"

"I *am* free. That would be neat."

I reached out to touch her hand, then withdrew. We weren't even on a first date.

I suggested that we go to an early show of the movie of *Cat on a Hot Tin Roof* and then have dinner afterwards.

"Do you like spaghetti?" asked Doris.

"Yes."

"Well, if you're ready to live dangerously," she said, "I

119

could make it for us after the movie. With just a simple tomato sauce and a few little things in it. And a salad and homemade bread. That way I can walk Kita not too late. Would you mind?"

"No, it would be great." I offered to bring dessert.

I felt touched by Doris's offer to make dinner, although it sounded awfully vegetarian. I was suspicious of the "few little things" she would put in the tomato sauce. With packaged foods, at least I knew what the ingredients were.

On the morning of our date, I bought two coffee and two chocolate eclairs for dessert, and I decided to get flowers for Doris.

I lingered over the array of choices at the florist's. Roses seemed too romantic for a first date, and carnations too ordinary. I also excluded all the exotic flowers with that jungle look I detested—flowers that had big leaves with sick-looking spots, or huge petals with large, fuzzy centers and no aroma. And flowers that looked obscene, as if a miniature tongue or penis were sticking out, or carnivorous, as if they might reach out suction-cupped leaves to eat the flesh of someone sleeping.

I settled on a bunch of yellow and white freesia, for their delicate fragrance.

"How did you know?" Doris exclaimed, when I gave them to her. She kissed me on the cheek. "Freesia are my absolute favorites."

Kita jumped up on me, barking and wagging his tail.

"Down, Kita!" said Doris. "He's friendly, but he has to learn manners. I named him for Nikita Khrushchev."

I enjoyed seeing *Cat on a Hot Tin Roof*, with Elizabeth Taylor in a nightgown, playing Maggie. When Burl Ives, as Big Daddy, pounded the bed and said, here was where a marriage was made or broken, I mentally filed away the line.

"Do you know the second-most-dangerous thing you can give to a dog?" I asked Doris later, while we were walking Kita after the movie.

"The *second*-most-dangerous thing for a dog? What a strange question. Is it fish, because of all the little bones?"

"Chicken bones," I said. "I only know it because my

father's a vet." I didn't want her to think I was showing off.

"All right, Andre Schulman, are you going to tell me the *first*-most dangerous thing for a dog?"

"Rubber." I felt proud to have something I could teach her. "Anything with rubber in it. Like erasers or rubber bands, or those rubber cat-head toys, if the dog's big enough to swallow it.

I also told her about *Ideal Marriage*'s advice on which types of lavender compounds to use in the bath—that genital odors were diminished by acids, such as a *"Vinaigre de toilette* prepared with lavender," but were heightened by alkalis, such as a lavender water fixed with tincture of musk, which, like soap, accentuated personal odors. I smiled to myself, picturing Jessica bathing in a lavender water fixed with an alkali, repelling men with her heightened genital odors.

Doris's dinner was better than I'd expected. Her home-made bread tasted great, and her spaghetti contained nothing that gave me trouble getting down, like lumps of cooked tomato.

"Do you think Big Daddy was right," she asked, "when he said that sex is the most important thing in a marriage?"

"Well, I don't know if it's the *most* important thing. But it's certainly important. Maybe if it's missing, that makes it become more important. What do *you* think?" I preferred to get her view first and then react to it.

"I think sex in marriage can be really neat," said Doris. "Kind of secret, special neat. A lot better than sex *out* of marriage, which is a rotten idea. You understand, I'm not judging anyone else. I'm only talking about my own standards. Andre, I'm sorry if they disappoint you."

"No, you've got to be true to yourself." But I *was* disappointed. She was the only girl I knew with her own apartment.

After dinner, Doris washed the dishes and I dried. As I dried them, I imagined that Jessica and I were doing the dishes together, our fingers touching each time she handed off a plate or glass to me. Then I felt disappointed when the dishes were done and reality returned.

121

"I had better let you get to sleep," I said. It was 11:00 o'clock. The later I stayed, the fewer buses would be running.

"Thank you for a lovely evening," said Doris.

"Thank you for a fine dinner," I responded, *lovely* feeling wrong in my mouth.

I reached out to shake hands good-night, and while holding her hand in mine, it seemed natural to lean over and kiss Doris.

Kissing her felt good. But I missed Jessica's kisses, her subtle movements along my mouth, the light touch of her hand caressing my neck, and the smell of her fragrance. It was like freesia, I realized.

I made another date with Doris for the following Saturday to see a matinee of Shaw's *Saint Joan*. I had written a paper on it for junior-year English.

Doris again offered to make dinner for us. This time, she would cook lamb chops. "I can't keep pushing vegetables on you," she said. "I never heard anyone say they're the way to a man's heart.

"Maybe not," I agreed. "But your spaghetti was good," too."

"I like chamber music more than symphonies," Doris said over dinner on Saturday. "Chamber music is purer. You can hear each instrument talking to the others."

"Hmm," I said, concentrating on the lamb chops, chewing on the narrow, crispy parts along the sides of the bone.

Chamber music bored me, I thought. It was too quiet. I preferred symphonies and concertos, especially the fast movements—*allegros, prestos, molto vivaces*. But maybe I could learn to appreciate chamber music. I felt open to change.

I drew the line, though, when Doris started praising Pablo Casals' marriage.

"It must be wonderful for his wife to be living with his music every day," said Doris. "And to know she was helping behind the scenes, letting him devote himself to bringing his music to the world."

"Doris, he's *sixty* years older than her. She's got to be more of a nursemaid than a wife to him. Casals may be a great musician, but it was immoral of him to marry a woman so much younger. Imagine them in ten years. Even in five. She'll still be near her sexual peak, while he'll, he'll need someone to carry his cello on stage for him. If Casals wants to recapture his youth, let him do it through his music, not by marrying someone young enough to be his granddaughter."

I stopped, sensing I was running-on too much.

"I'm sorry," I said. "I just wouldn't want you to do something like that and ruin your own chance for a full life."

"Andre, that's so sweet of you."

The next Saturday I took Doris out to dinner at Pierre au Tunnel, which my mother had suggested, as a restaurant that was French and romantic, but not "outrageously expensive."

I ordered *coq au vin* and felt sophisticated eating it at a candle-lit table, with waiters speaking French. But *coq au vin* seemed to me just bony chicken in a heavy sauce, with a shriveled-up stewed tomato. I regretted having passed up the entrecote with *pommes frites*.

After dinner, we went back to Doris's apartment and sat on her sofa bed, eating dark chocolate-chip cookies she had baked that afternoon and that were still warm and moist. The chocolate bits stuck to the roof of my mouth, making their taste linger pleasantly.

"I think Kita needs worming," I said, looking over at the dog. "You can tell by the way he slides along the floor on his rear end."

"Yes, I've wondered about that," said Doris. "As the son of a vet, what rates do you charge for advice?"

"Well, this *is* a home visit. They do run higher, you know. Two of your cookies, or one kiss and a cookie for the road."

"I'll take the kiss," said Doris. She leaned toward me and, when I kissed her, snuggled against me. I took off my shoes. "I don't want to get your couch dirty," I said, then lay back on her sofa-bed and drew her down beside me.

Recalling *Ideal Marriage*'s saying that a man must embrace

123

a woman with dominant virility, I reached a hand under the back of Doris's blouse and kissed her. This time, I used my tongue, and she responded with hers. But when I snaked my hand around her body toward her breasts, she stopped my hand and held it.

"*Sometime* I would like it very much if you touched my breasts. But not tonight. Is that okay?"

"Of course," I said, meaning it and withdrawing my hand. "I want you to feel comfortable with me." Even though my groin ached, I felt proud of the pain. It marked a step forward for me.

Seeing Doris became a comfortable weekly routine. I liked her a lot. Sometimes we went out. Other times we studied together at her place and then made dinner. She taught me how to cook with garlic and ginger, blanch vegetables so they didn't become limp, and make salad dressing, adding a little sugar for softening. With Doris, I felt I was learning about the non-sexual aspects of marriage—not only cooking, but choosing furniture, decorating an apartment, and acting as a couple with friends. If only I loved her, I thought, my life would be perfect.

On a bright Sunday in mid-April Doris drove us up to Bear Mountain Lake in her 1947 black Chrysler. Its rear end rode higher than the front, making the car look as if it was always heading into the ground.

We walked around the lake until a cold breeze made us switch to a trail in the woods. While we walked, Doris pointed out spring flowers—buttercups and dandelions, violets and coltsfoot—and I tried to take an interest in them.

Around six-thirty, I gathered up pieces of wood and built a fire in a barbecue pit. This was the moment I'd been waiting for. I cooked steak on a grill and potatoes and onions in a pan, often adding more butter to the pan to keep the potatoes and onions from sticking and turning black. I liked the feel of their coming unstuck under my long fork when I added the butter and the smell of the food cooking. Nor did I mind having to move whenever the wind changed direction and blew smoke into my nose and eyes. It was all part of cooking out.

Everything tasted wonderful to me—the charcoal-grilled steak, the pan-fried onions and potatoes, well salted, the Cokes I'd brought along from home, even the salad Doris had made to add a touch of health.

After dinner we lay down on a blanket and looked up at a sky full of stars, not just the two or three visible in New York. I savored the combination of pleasures—kissing Doris while looking at the stars and still tasting the steak, potatoes, and onions.

How beautiful the stars were, I thought. Generations had been linked together through the ages by their all viewing the same nighttime sky—until around the 1930s, when airplane lights started appearing and then those of helicopters.

"Aren't the stars incredible!" said Doris. "That's how I feel when I listen to chamber music. Each instrument stands out individually, playing its own part, just like each star tonight. To me, a symphony is more like the Milky Way—all blurred together. Do you see what I mean?"

"I do," I said. "But I still prefer symphonies. They may be blurrier than chamber music, but they're also more powerful. Like all the stars in a galaxy, each instrument in a symphony is not only itself, but part of something larger. Probably I'm just at a lower level of musical development than you," I added, sensing I might have been arguing just to argue.

Back at Doris's apartment, we cuddled on her sofa-bed.

"I hope you know that my keeping my virginity is nothing against you," she said.

"I do know," I said.

"But I would feel cheap if I slept with someone and then didn't marry him. I'd feel I was cheating my future husband of something he has a right to. And I know it would show in my face. Everyone would see that I wasn't a virgin. Even if they didn't see it, *I* would know. I'd have to go and teach in some remote women's college, like Wheaten. Please don't be angry at me."

"I'm not." I knew that Doris was being sincere. "If you want to stay a virgin," I said, "don't let anyone talk you out of it, including me. But promise me one thing—if you do stay a virgin, that you'll masturbate regularly." I told her about *Ideal Marriage*'s saying that regular masturbation prevented the membrane around the hymen from growing tough, making eventual intercourse more difficult. "I don't want your staying a virgin to make it more painful for you when you do get married."

"I promise," she said. "But I'm concerned about *you*. Isn't it painful for a man to get all excited and do nothing about it?"

"Sometimes," I said. "But it's worth it to me to be with you."

"I want to be good for you in that way, too," said Doris. She led Kita into the bathroom by his collar and closed the door on him. Then she unzipped the fly of my jeans and started caressing my penis.

I reached down and caressed her, too, searching for her clitoris. I mentally scanned the diagram of female genitalia in *Ideal Marriage*. But all I could picture was a bunch of sacs and canals. Then I closed my eyes, as when listening to music, and found it just in time. I came right before she did.

"Thank you," I said, afterward. "You can't imagine how good that felt."

"I'm happy I could do it for you. It was good for me, too."

I stretched out contentedly, listening to Kita lapping up water from the toilet. It was the first time I'd ever brought a girl to orgasm, or she had brought me to it.

"Andre, I've been thinking," Doris said, after a while. "What we did felt *too* good to me. Like I was playing games with my virginity. I was keeping it only technically, while doing things that I know belong only in marriage. This probably makes no sense to you, but I don't want to repeat it. I mean, I do want to, but I don't. Can you understand me?"

"Yes, I can. I don't want to make you feel bad with me. And I certainly don't want you to have to go teach at Wheaten, unless you want to."

In a way I felt relieved. I didn't want to marry Doris, but to get her to sleep with me and then *not* marry her would be too cruel.

"Doris," I said, "I respect your attitude about sex. And knowing it, I'd feel awful if I led you to do something you regretted. Or if one time we *both* slipped, and then it was too late. You mean too much to me. I'd rather we just stay very close friends."

I thought it was kinder to take it on myself, saying that I respected her attitude about sex without marriage, instead of that I didn't want to marry her.

Later at home, it struck me that I had practically lost my virginity. It was only a matter of a few inches.

I thought about the Passover chant "*Dayenu.*" It celebrated the journey of the ancient Jews out of Egypt to the promised land. Each verse described a particular leg of that journey and told God that, even if He had brought them only thus far and no farther, *dayenu*—it would have been enough. I tried applying it to Doris. If she had merely replaced Bradshaw in my life, but had kept things platonic between us, it would have been enough. If she and I had kissed and necked, but she had stayed fully dressed, it would have been enough. If she had let me touch her bare breasts, but not go any further, it would have been enough. That we had petted to orgasm, but hadn't had intercourse, was more than enough.

On the other hand, the ancient Jews got to complete their journey, despite all the *dayenus* along the way.

Chapter Nine

GOOSE DOWN

> The soul of this arch-lover [Don Juan]
> was not seeking the base triumph of snatching
> and throwing away, but ever and only the
> ecstasy of giving the joy of love.
>
> *Ideal Marriage*, Page 9.

I GOT A job over spring vacation in the pillow department at Bloomingdale's. Every day, I found myself asking customers the same question—"Would you like duck down or goose down?"

The pillow department was in an alcove about twenty by twenty-five feet. Bins of pillows stood in the center, racks with sample pillows ran along the walls, and a glassed-in display case held specialty items—bolsters, travel pillows, and miniature neck supports looking like little toilet-training seats.

After my experience working at Davega's—when I'd laced up a pair of ice skates on the wrong feet of a six-year-old girl—I was determined this time to do a good job. I persuaded the floor manager to let me take home a sample of each pillow so I could advise customers "more informedly." And I went to the library and read about pillows, then practiced the terminology. "Pure Balkan white goose down." "A finer thread count in the ticking." "Higher fill power gives greater loft." I also coined the term "flip rate," for how frequently I needed to turn over a pillow to keep it from becoming too warm.

I enjoyed the work. I would arrive early and walk around my alcove, touching the various pillows. If no one was there, I would hold a few pillows against my cheek, trying to feel differences among them—the softness and malleability of down, the slight nubbiness from the quills in the feather pillows, and the way the foam rubber pillows bounced back when I lifted my head from them.

I liked sharing in the happiness of the pillow shoppers and sensing they appreciated the care I was taking with them.

"Do you prefer sleeping with your head elevated, or level with your body?" I'd ask. Depending on the answer, I would recommend firmer or looser pillows.

I urged customers to squeeze the pillows and lie down on one of the beds with a floor sample for a tryout. I even felt a kinship with the pillow fetishists—the regulars who never bought anything, but kept dropping in to feel the pillows furtively. It wasn't far from what I did myself, I thought, although for research purposes. And when my feet got tired from standing too long, I went over to the electric shoe buffer, took off my shoes, and buffed my feet on it, massaging them thoroughly.

On my third day at work, a slim woman with dark curly hair came into my alcove and walked up to me briskly.

"I need two nice pillows," she said.

"Do you prefer duck down or goose down?" I asked automatically.

"Are those my choices?" she said, teasingly. "What about swan down, or dog down?" She had a sly smile, bright-red fingernails, and an upturned nose like a ski jump.

"I'm sorry, but we don't carry them," I said, wondering whether dogs had down. I hadn't thought so, but her question made me uncertain.

"Are you in high school?" she asked.

"Yes, I'm a senior." I hoped that the "senior" part sounded at least a little grown-up. "How about *you*—are you in college?"

"Well, I was at college last weekend, for my fifth reunion." She smiled. "Does that count as being in college?"

I calculated. She had to be about twenty-six or twenty-seven—ten years older than me.

"I want to replace two pillows," she said. "I didn't replace them before, because I was staying at my boyfriend's apartment. But Chester and I are breaking up." She laughed. "That's why I need new pillows. Chester has nice soft pillows, but I don't think I should stay with a man just for his pillows. Do you?"

"That makes sense," I said, liking to agree with her.

I showed her a range of pillows—from foam rubber up through feathers, feathers and down mixed, duck down, goose down, and finally, imported goose down—pointing out the incremental advantages of each.

"Why not try out a bunch of pillows before deciding?" I suggested. "What matters isn't what *I* say about them, but how *you feel.* Anyway," I lowered my voice, "I think it's fun to try out pillows."

"Oh, me, too."

She laughed, then spread out several pillows on the counter and put her head down on each. She declared that she liked the goose down best, the *Balkan* goose down. "It feels soft and smooth," she said, "but not *too* soft. Not so soft that my head sinks down to the bottom."

"Well, the Balkan white goose down does have the most loft," I said. "And it has the lowest flip rate—it stays cool the longest, so you don't have to keep turning the pillow over all the time."

"But is goose down the most sensual?" She smiled at me. "Is that the pillow *you* would choose for sensuality?"

"Well..". I said. I felt at a loss, as when I'd go blank on an exam question. "Yes, yes, it is the most sensual," I declared. "Because goose down, the Balkan white goose down, especially, comes with the finest thread count on the cover ticking. The finer the thread count, the silkier the pillow feels."

"You've convinced me," she said. "I'll take two. Do you know, you're the best pillow salesman I've ever met?"

"Thank you very much," I said. "Well, you're the nicest customer I've ever met. I'm not just saying that, I mean it." I

131

felt attracted to her.

"I once knew a man with *fabulous* pillows," she said. "He had big, soft pillows you could sink right into. If you ever want to seduce a girl, put elegant pillows on your bed. Remember that—it's Gloria's law. I'm Gloria, Gloria Kelsey." She held out her hand and I shook it.

"I'm Andre Schulman. I'm pleased to meet you. And thank you for Gloria's law."

I realized that, if I wanted to see her again, I had to act fast before she left.

"Miss Kelsey," I said, after writing up her order (calling her *Gloria* didn't seem right with a customer, especially one older than me), "Miss Kelsey, I would very much like to see you again. Could I invite you out for dinner sometime, like this Friday or Saturday?"

She looked at me, and I tried to meet her eyes.

"Yes," she said, "Friday would work for me. But I insist we go Dutch. I can't let you spend your vacation earnings on me. And call me *Gloria. Miss Kelsey* sounds like one of your schoolteachers. Or is that your fantasy about me?"

I felt excited. Gloria had just broken up with her boyfriend, and *Ideal Marriage* said that grief could arouse sexual emotions and a longing to console or be consoled. Maybe I'd be Gloria's consoler.

On Friday evening, I put on my blue suit and a blue-and-gray paisley tie. The tie looked to me like spermatozoa, but my mother had said it was "sophisticated." I also took along two Fourex condoms, just in case. They were packed in translucent plastic containers of sapphire blue, my favorite color. It reminded me of the evening sky in the West, luminous between sunset and dark. I held one of the Four-X containers up to my bedside lamp, to appreciate the richness of the blue when it was lit from behind like a stained-glass window.

Then I bit into the container slightly. I wanted it to open easily, but not so easily that the liquid around the condoms

132

seeped out into my pocket. My chances of sleeping with Gloria might be slightly enhanced since a thunderstorm was approaching. According to *Ideal Marriage,* "the atmosphere of an approaching storm has a particularly exciting and disturbing effect sexually," but only "before thunder and lightning have begun." If I did lose my virginity, it might help me to get Jessica back, making me smoother in how I behaved with her.

At 7:29, I rang the bell at Gloria's apartment on Lexington and 32nd Street. I thought it politer to arrive a minute early than a minute late, and waiting until exactly 7:30 would have seemed too precise.

There was a bottle of wine and some food on her coffee table.

"I thought we'd have a drink here first, and some *hors d'oeuvres,*" she said, airily. "It looks like a storm's coming. Would you mind if we wait to go out till it passes?"

"No, not a bit," I said. On the contrary, I thought.

Gloria looked sophisticated to me, all in yellow, except for bright-red lipstick and fingernails. She had on a yellow skirt and top with a heart-shaped neckline, which seemed to lead my eyes downward as if following a pointer in the Planetarium.

"A glass of wine?" she asked. "It's a *Pouilly Fuissé.* Or would you prefer something else—sherry or scotch, or a vodka and tonic?"

"No, the wine is fine. Thank you." I wanted to say, "the *Pouilly Fuissé,*" but was afraid of mispronouncing it.

I sat down on the couch at the end opposite the chair Gloria was sitting on. To make conversation, I thought of asking her what she had majored in at college, but I feared she would think me childish. Then I saw a weak flash of lightning.

"Gloria, I'm sorry about you and Chester breaking up," I said. I wanted to console her before the storm arrived. "I mean, I'm happy because I get to see you, but I'm sorry if you're going through a tough time. Sometimes, talking about it with someone can make you feel better. While I'm just a high-school senior, I'd be happy to listen."

"Andre, I have a different idea."

133

Gloria moved over to the couch and took my hand. "I have a confession," she said. "I hope it doesn't shock you. Before you came, I was fantasizing about how you look naked. I would like to go to bed with you. Does that shock you, Andre? Am I being too bold?"

"No. No. If you're being too bold, then I'm glad you're being too bold. I mean, it's just the right amount of bold." I sensed I was babbling.

"Good," said Gloria. "I like to be direct. If someone can't accept it, *tant pis*. That's French. It means 'too bad.'"

She led me into her bedroom. "After all," she said, laughing, "it's only fair that my pillow salesman gets to try out my new pillows *first*. Why don't you undress while I use the bathroom."

As soon as Gloria closed the bathroom door, I took out the Fourex container that I'd bitten into and tucked it under the mattress within arm's reach. Then I hung up my jacket, peeled off my shirt, tie, and pants, and dove under the covers. I kept on my undershorts for modesty, in case Gloria kept on her underwear.

Lightening flashed outside. It seemed closer now. Like Mao Tse Tung, I thought, I was about to make a great leap forward. I sucked in my stomach, hoping not to disappoint Gloria's fantasy of how I'd look naked.

I heard water running in the bathroom in spurts. Why was it running in *spurts*? I wondered. Was it somehow connected with "feminine hygiene," a term that intrigued me?

I sang to myself the theme from Beethoven's Violin Concerto. But I sang it to the words, "It's going to happen, it's going to happen, it's going to happen, *soon*."

The water stopped running in the bathroom. Gloria came out, wrapped only in a pink towel. She lit a candle on top of her bureau, then turned off the lights, shed her towel, and slipped into bed next to me.

"Do you plan to keep those on?" she asked, running her fingers along the front of my undershorts.

I pulled off my undershorts and dropped them over the edge

of the bed, feeling almost *too* excited. Then I caressed Gloria's face, shoulders, and stomach, avoiding her breasts and pubic area at first, as *Ideal Marriage* advised.

Gloria took my hand and placed it between her legs.

"You remind me of an old boyfriend I had," she said, laughing. "He treated me as if I didn't exist below the waist."

I moved a finger upward, found her clitoris, and began caressing it.

"Mmm, that's better," she said. Gloria stretched her head backwards and reached a hand down to my penis, fluttering over and around it. I feared coming too soon. To hold off, I mentally named all the bedding accessories I could think of—sheets and pillow cases, dust ruffles, duvet covers, bolsters and mattress pads.

Kissing Gloria to divert her attention, I groped under the mattress for the Four-X. As I began opening it, she stopped me.

"You don't need that, I've got my diaphragm. Now, come here!"

I climbed over her and she guided me in. I pushed in as far as I could, to make sure. Then I realized I'd done it—I'd lost my virginity. It was the happiest moment of my life.

Now I would concentrate on *Gloria's* pleasure. I supported myself on my knees and elbows, not wanting to be one of those inconsiderate men who rested their weight on a woman during intercourse.

Gloria was howling softly, like a dog hearing a siren.

"Am I hurting you?" I asked.

"No. Relax, I won't break." She pulled me down against her. "I want to feel your weight."

"I love you," I said, swept up in feeling for her and thinking it wrong not to say, "I love you" to someone I was making love with.

"I'm *coming*," said Gloria. She screamed and bit my shoulder. "Come! Hurry!" She reached under my testicles and stroked them insistently.

I felt I was going to come. I was almost there—

Then suddenly, I wasn't. Feeling a finger shooting up my

rear end, I leapt off of her, imagining her fingernail scratching my insides. A moment later, I came.

"I'm sorry!" I said, spurting over her bed, unable to stop. "I'm *terribly* sorry." I felt humiliated. I turned onto my stomach, trying to concentrate my spurting in one spot.

Gloria got a towel from the bathroom and wiped me off, along with the bed.

"I thought you'd find a little finger up there exciting," she said. "Do you think maybe it's an acquired taste?"

I felt desolate. If only I'd come a second earlier, or had anticipated her finger in my rear end and had stayed inside her until I came.

On the other hand, everything had been fine until the final second. Next time, I would expect her finger in me and not be thrown by it.

I reached out to her. *Ideal Marriage* said that too many men just turned over and went to sleep after intercourse, neglecting the woman's need for "after-play," with caresses and sweet words. In after-play, a man proved whether or not he was "an erotically civilized adult." That was what I wanted to be, I thought—an erotically civilized adult.

I caressed Gloria's arms, face, and shoulders, feeling shy again. I kept sneaking glances at her body, as if looking was wrong, even now. If I had finished inside her, I thought, I would have been bolder.

"You're beautiful," I said to her.

"Thanks," she said.

Her bed was luxurious. The sheets and pillow cases had lace ruffles with tiny holes, and instead of blankets, she had a comforter. It felt smooth against my face, unlike my blanket at home, which felt scratchy whenever it slid up over my top sheet. A three-inch TV set sat on the end table on my side of Gloria's bed. If she fell asleep first, I might watch *Cat Women of the Moon* on the *Late Late Show*, the only thing on after 1:00 a.m.

"Do you know, you're wonderful?" I said, touching her elbow.

"I'm starving!" she said, and sat up. "Is it okay if we don't go out in the rain? I've got Camembert and a French baguette. And we can drink the rest of the *Pouilly Fuissé*."

"Staying in would be *great*." It would make it easier for me to make love with her again, I thought, determined next time to finish inside her. But I felt a bit apprehensive about the Camembert. I had never tried any, because whenever my father brought some home, our whole refrigerator smelled bad.

"Maybe you want to take a shower first," said Gloria. "You must be all sticky. There's an extra bathrobe you can use. Chester left it."

"Yes, I would like to take a shower." I had wanted to take one earlier, but had thought it would be crude to leave Gloria right after we'd made love.

While showering, I reflected that, when I got married, I wanted to have at least a queen-sized bed. Twin beds, like my parents had, eliminated all spontaneity. You had to decide in advance when you were going to make love, then cross over from one bed to the other to do it, and cross back again to your own bed to sleep. But until tonight, I had never considered a king-sized bed. It had seemed too extravagant—something for movie stars, pimps, or pro basketball players.

After my shower, Gloria and I sat in our bathrobes in her dining alcove, eating Camembert and French bread and drinking Pouilly Fuissé. It seemed romantic and adult to be sitting together in our bathrobes after making love. And the Camembert tasted good and wasn't at all smelly.

Seeing Gloria in her bathrobe, I recalled an essay by Bertrand Russell. It mentioned an order of nuns who always wore bathing suits when taking a bath, lest the good Lord see them naked. Apparently, said Russell, the nuns thought of the Deity as a peeping Tom who could see through bathroom walls, but was foiled by bathing suits.

Gloria talked about her work at the Ford Foundation, deciding to whom to give grants.

It was a great job, she said. "I have no pressure. No one tells me to hurry up, or we won't accept your money."

While she talked, I imagined that I could still feel the imprint of her finger inside my rear end. The thought excited me again.

Gloria looked at her watch. "It's only ten-thirty, but I'm pooped," she said. "I'm going to send you home. I don't want your parents saying, 'Who's that wicked, older woman keeping our son out till all hours?'"

"They won't," I said. "I'll call them and say I'm out at an all-night progressive party." I desperately wanted to stay and make love with Gloria again, to complete it. "I'm not one of those guys who goes to bed with a girl and then runs off and leaves her. But *you* can go to sleep, if you want to—the bed's big enough that you won't even know I'm there."

"A gentleman doesn't make a fuss when a lady says she's pooped," said Gloria. She gathered up my clothes and handed them to me. "Here, take these into the bathroom and get dressed. Okay?"

No, it wasn't *okay*.

"Gloria, wait!" I said. "There's something I want to do first." I dropped my clothes back onto the chair and walked over to her. She was sitting on the bed, still in her bathrobe.

"Now, lie back, and don't argue!" I said. I pushed her back gently and opened her bathrobe. "I'm going to go down on you."

I put my tongue into her vagina without waiting for permission.

"*Okay*," she said, with a lilt.

I moved my tongue in and out, and around what I imagined was her clitoris, thinking back to my practice with the chocolate turkey.

"Mmm," said Gloria. "That's good!" She kept making sounds of pleasure.

I recalled my mother's saying that my father didn't like to go down on her. In a way, I felt I was making up for her deprivation, even if with another woman.

To vary my tongue movements, I added semicircles and figure eights. Then after coming up briefly for air, I switched to football plays—button hooks, down-and-outs, reverses, off-tackle slants, safety blitzes. Making up variations distracted me from how tired my tongue felt. Recalling the phrase, "corkscrew tongue," I tried curling my tongue while moving it around.

"I'm coming!" yelled Gloria. "It's strong!" I felt her writhing about, and I tried to stay with her. Then she lay back and pulled me up onto her.

"Now it's *your* turn," she said, with her usual lilt.

I came quickly, then stayed deep inside her. I wanted to take no chance of popping out again.

Dayenu, I thought. The final *dayenu*. My journey was complete. I felt myself relaxing, savoring the happy ending.

"Did I wear out your poor little tongue?" asked Gloria. "Poor tongue, it was working so hard. I'm sorry it took me a while to get back in the mood."

"You don't have to apologize," I said. "I *liked* doing it."

At least, I liked the *result*, I thought, hoping my tongue was still well attached.

"Admit it," said Gloria. "You were a virgin, weren't you? You can't fool *me*—I have a nose for virgins."

"Well, actually, I was... I was halfway a non-virgin."

"Hon, it's the *second* half that counts."

"Yes, you're right. I see that now." It was like Bradshaw's second rebirth, I thought. It had made him realize that he'd probably only imagined the first.

"Get dressed now," said Gloria. "You can take another shower first, but I want you out of here in fifteen minutes. I need my sleep, and I'm going to sleep *alone*."

Leaving didn't bother me now. I showered and dressed and prepared to take my first steps out into the world as a non-virgin.

"One thing before I leave," I said. I had hesitated about mentioning something so personal, but it seemed only right to tell her, if it might save her from unnecessary illness. And now that we'd made love, I could talk about intimate things without its being crude.

"Gloria," I said, "I've been reading a book by this Dutch gynecologist, Van der Velde." (I hurried along, knowing Gloria was waiting for me to go.) "He says that women should urinate frequently and thoroughly. Otherwise, their bladder gets overloaded, and the urine decomposes inside. That can cause chronic inflammatory lesions.

"I'm sorry to be so personal, but I thought you'd prefer knowing."

"Thank you," said Gloria. "I'll remember that—frequently and thoroughly. Now, go! I'm wiped." She yawned and opened the door for me.

I started through it. "Would you like to go out next Saturday, or Friday?" I asked. She shouldn't think I'd been interested in her only for sex.

"I can't," she said. "I'm going skiing next weekend."

"Then how about the following weekend?"

"I don't know yet. I might be away then, too. You could call me around the middle of the week. "But don't wait for me, Andre. You've got to feel free to make other plans."

On the bus home, I found a place behind one of the few seats with a heater under it. That seemed a good omen. I took off my shoes, stretched out my feet against the heater, and enjoyed that delicious moment when my feet turned warm before starting to burn.

At Friends Meeting that Sunday, I silently thanked the Quaker Spirit for answering my prayer to let me lose my virginity. I vowed to use that loss in a worthy manner, in aid of making a good marriage. If Jessica ever gave me another chance, I would know how to act with her, not just sexually but in general, radiating confidence.

The next time I made love with Gloria, I would enjoy every moment of it. The first time, I had simply wanted to get it done.

Ideal Marriage spoke of the delight of the "vaginal clasp, in its pillowy softness and delicacy, its intense warmth." Next time, I wanted to focus on that clasp and enjoy it. I would also try to keep Gloria from biting me again. Although *Ideal Marriage* said that women were more addicted to love bites than men, I hadn't liked being bitten. It had hurt.

Gloria had said to call her around the middle of the week. I phoned her on Wednesday evening at nine-thirty, figuring she would have finished dinner but not yet gone to bed.

"Andre, I enjoyed our evening together," she said. "And you'll always be my favorite pillow salesman. If I ever buy pillows again, I'll look for you in Bloomingdale's. But it won't work for us as lovers. You need to find a girl your own age."

"No, age doesn't matter," I said, then searched for arguments. "Actually, it's *better* that you're older. Women live longer than men."

"Believe me, Andre, it won't work."

"I believe you that it won't work if you don't *want* it to. Please, tell me why? It could help me in the future."

"Okay," said Gloria. "But I'm telling you only because you're pressuring me. The truth is that, after I sleep with a man, I always grade the experience. It's just something I do, to keep my perspective. At first, I gave you a 'C-Minus.' Then after you went down on me, I raised it to a 'C.' Or maybe a 'C-Plus,' for your working so hard. But I've made a 'B' my minimum grade for seeing a man again. It lets me nip unpromising involvements right away, before anyone gets hurt. Believe me, Andre, it's nothing against you."

"Thanks for telling me," I said. After all, I *had* asked her.

I felt terrible. Only a "C-Plus." But how could I argue with her grading?

"What about a make-up exam?" I asked. "Like with the College Boards. You can take them twice and count only your best score. Couldn't you do the same with me, give me another chance in a few months?"

Gloria laughed. "Andre, I'm sorry. If I make an exception for *you*, I'd have to do it for everyone else who scored a 'C-Plus.' Look at the bright side." (The lilt came back in her voice.) "Your next girl friend will benefit from your experience with me. If you really think about it, I've been good for you."

141

I went to bed, gloomy about the "C-Plus" Gloria had given me. Then I remembered the day that our new English teacher had come into class at the beginning of my junior year.

"My name is Jonathan Kaufman," he had said. "Most of you will get 'C's. 'C' is a decent grade. I give it if you have done all the assigned work. 'B's are only for something extra. And an 'A' is a rarity in my class. Some years I don't give any." He turned out to be the best teacher in the school.

Maybe a "C-Plus" was a decent grade, after all, I reflected, especially if Gloria marked on a curve and I was competing against older, more experienced men. It might even be the highest grade she had ever given to a virgin.

Chapter Ten

GRADUATION

It is an enormous error to regard perfect technique in sexual intercourse as *an end in itself.* They who make this mistake will find the same disappointments and disillusionments, with this expert knowledge, as without it.

Ideal Marriage, page 321.

ON MY LAST day of work at Bloomingdale's, the bedding manager asked me to "step into" his office.

What had I done wrong? I wondered. Had a customer complained about me, or had I been caught massaging my feet on the shoe-buffing machine?

"Sit down," said the bedding manager, pointing to a chair across from his desk. He picked up a few sheets of paper. "According to my records, your performance has been excellent. Several of our customers have commended your helpfulness and your depth of knowledge of the merchandise. Those qualities are rare enough in a full-time employee, let alone a temporary employee like yourself. I think congratulations are in order." He leaned across the desk to shake hands.

I felt ecstatic. He had told me I did a good job.

"Upon my recommendation," the bedding manager continued, "Bloomingdale's is pleased to make you an offer of permanent employment after you graduate from high school. Or should you go on to college, we can offer you employment during the summers and the likelihood—but mind you, no promises—of joining our executive-training program upon obtaining your degree."

"Thank you," I said. "Thank you very much. I probably *will* go to college...if I get in. But I'd *love* to work at Bloomingdale's again.

On my way back to the pillow alcove, I first circled the entire bedding floor, surveying my realm. I wanted to imprint it all into memory. A wonderful future lay ahead of me—a job every summer at Bloomingdale's and then, if I wanted it, the chance to become an executive.

Before leaving work that final day, I used my employee's discount to buy two Balkan white goose-down pillows. One I would sleep on at home. The other I would keep fresh for whomever I eventually married. I pressed one of the pillows against my face, imagining Jessica's head resting on her pillow next to mine. And I pictured us lying in bed together after making love—something I now knew how to do—each of us gazing adoringly at the other.

While it was only a tiny thing, I wondered whether, if Jessica ever felt herself evenly divided between returning to me or not, her knowing that I'd gotten great pillows for us might make the difference. Sometimes, such a little thing might sway someone in one direction or another.

Bloomingdale's job offer helped ease my tension during the final week of waiting for college-decision letters. I felt that I now had my own equivalent of a "safe school." If none of the places I had applied to accepted me, I could work at Bloomingdale's, while applying to other, easier colleges.

Life was also looking up for my father.

"I have an announcement to make, everyone," he declared over dessert one evening, his eyes twinkling. "I am finally about to realize my life-long desire as a veterinarian—to stop treating cats. I have reached the point where I can afford to eliminate them from my practice and still make a decent living.

In the future, I'll treat only dogs and a few exotics for variety. I am looking for a vet who prefers cats, so we can trade off our patients.

"Congratulations, dear," said my mother.

"I'm so happy for you, Daddy," said Alice. She went up to him and threw her arms around his neck.

"That's wonderful, Dad!" I said. "Congratulations from me, too. But what made you decide right *now*?"

My father said that he had met a cancer researcher at a luncheon on zoonoses, diseases transmittable from animals to humans. The researcher had mentioned that he allowed no cats in his own home because of the virulence of the feline leukemia virus. While admitting that the virus had not *yet* been shown to be transmittable to humans, he said that he was playing it safe.

"I have decided to do likewise," said my father. "While I don't believe in running scared in life, neither do I consider it responsible for me to subject my family, or myself for that matter, to unnecessary risks.

"I've also come to realize," he continued, "that it's a poor idea for the same veterinarian to be treating both cats and dogs. Each of them can tell when one of the other's been on my examining table. It drives them up the wall. It makes them both more afraid of the vet."

I felt thankful that I'd no longer risk getting feline leukemia from helping my father, or shaking hands with him after he'd handled a cat. But it was a risk that I'd previously been unaware of. I wondered now whether my risk would end once my father stopped treating cats, or was it cumulative over a lifetime, like exposure to radiation?

"Bloomingdale's," I kept repeating to myself, trying to stay calm on the day the decision-letters from colleges arrived.

Cornell, my third choice, accepted me. Harvard, my second choice, turned me down. And Swarthmore, my first choice, put me on the waiting list, then three weeks later accepted me, relieving me from going up to Cornell in the frozen North.

I kept re-reading Swarthmore's admission letter, delighting in it.

But what if I flunked out? Since Swarthmore had accepted me only from its waiting list, I was surely near the bottom of the class. I would have to work extra hard just to pass, let alone get into the honors program. I would be competing with all the National Merit Award winners and students on GE or Westinghouse scholarships.

A few days later, I was looking through the Swarthmore Catalogue on the bus home from school.

"You aren't planning to go to there, are you?" asked a woman sitting next to me.

"Well, I *might*." Although I'd already sent in my acceptance, her tone made me cautious.

"I don't want to frighten you," she said, "but are you aware that Swarthmore has the highest suicide rate of any college in the country?"

I hadn't been aware. When I'd visited Swarthmore in the fall, a student guide did mention that only seniors got keys to the college tower. She said that, after surviving three years at Swarthmore, they were less likely to jump, although a senior *had* jumped the previous spring during honors exams.

Luckily, I thought, I wasn't suicidal. But just in case I had any unconscious suicidal wishes, I always stood well back from the edges of subway platforms and building terraces.

Graduation at Mattoon was held in the evening, on the school roof six stories high. After raining for two days, the weather had cleared.

The senior class traditionally got to select their own speaker. We sent out invitations to Adlai Stevenson, John Steinbeck, Margaret Sanger, and Supreme Court Justices Black and Douglas. As a backup, we also invited Sidney Wolfe, an NYU sociology professor, who was a friend of one of the parents. A consultant on poverty and a self-styled Marxist, Professor Wolfe was the only speaker to accept.

We graduates-to-be sat on folding chairs in front of a makeshift platform with a lectern mounted on it. Behind the dias sat the Principal, Professor Wolfe, and the members of Mattoon's Board of Trustees, among them my father.

The senior boys wore blue suits. The girls wore dresses with widely varying necklines. Inhabitants of the taller, adjacent buildings leaned out of their windows and called down comments, mostly about the more revealingly-dressed girls.

The Principal opened the ceremonies by thanking the Board of Trustees "for wisely and patiently guiding Mattoon in its pursuit of excellence." I looked at my father proudly and saw him nod in acknowledgment.

Next, the Principal called each senior forward to receive a rolled-up piece of blank paper tied with a ribbon. The actual diplomas would be mailed later to avoid embarrassing the two seniors who had flunked courses and would have to go to summer school before graduating.

Professor Wolfe, plump and bearded, began his address by describing his work as a poverty consultant.

"Poverty is a growing field," he said. "A chance to do good and make money at the same time, if you get in on the ground floor." He recommended that we consider it.

"Our government has so grievously wronged the people," he continued—"killing the Rosenbergs, outlawing the Communist Party, strangling the unions through Taft-Hartley—that surely the people are justified in living off of the government in return."

Switching to foreign policy, he praised the Viet Minh's victory over the French at Dien Bien Phu and urged us to "resist the draft by whatever means are necessary."

As Professor Wolfe went on, cries of "Commie!" and "Go back to Russia!" came from the neighboring buildings. People threw down handfuls of dirt from window-sill flowerpots and a bowl of succotash. We all rushed indoors. I ran in a zig-zag pattern in case anyone was aiming at me.

The Principal adjourned graduation to the auditorium, where chairs were hastily set up and the lectern placed on the

147

stage.

"I apologize to everyone for the interruption," said the Principal. "Yet, as rude as it was, it once again demonstrates Mattoon's proud tradition of supporting freedom of speech, no matter how controversial. I want to publicly thank Dr. Wolfe for what I'm sure everyone could see and hear was a very stimulating speech. And now to conclude, I ask that everyone join with me in wishing our graduates well as they set out on their journeys through life."

I heard clapping behind me. Then to my embarrassment, I saw my father stand up, whisper to the Principal, and walk to the lectern.

"Dad, don't!" I begged, silently. "Please, let it pass."

I saw my classmates turning to look at me, and I wished I were anywhere else.

"I hadn't planned to speak this evening," said my father. "It would have been easier for me just to remain silent and swallow what Professor Wolfe has said to you. But I honestly don't believe that that would serve your best interests.

"I am sure that Professor Wolfe is a well-meaning man by his own lights. Yet, I submit to you that what matters is not whether you believe, as he does, that the United States Government is the Devil incarnate, or whether you believe, as I do, that our government is essentially well motivated.

"No. What matters is that, instead of telling you what to believe, educators should be urging you to think for yourselves and to guard against the half truths of anyone with a message to sell—whether demagogues of the left or of the right. And you should never be fooled by what title or degrees someone has or how passionately he or she speaks. It's what the person *says* that counts, and in assessing that, you should always use your own judgment. Remember that the ace of spades is the same ace of spades, whether you slam it down or lay it down quietly."

By the time my father finished, my embarrassment had changed to pride. He had spoken so calmly and intelligently. I wanted to join in the audience's applause for him, but I felt strange about applauding my own father in public, especially in front of my classmates.

At home later, I opened *Ideal Marriage* to its final page. I had saved it for after graduation as something to look forward to and as symbolic of my interest in the subject's not ending with high school.

The "true sense and significance" of ideal marriage "implies love," I read. "Voluptuous pleasure *alone*, however refined and varied, cannot bring real happiness, without that solace to the soul which humanity desires, and *must* forever seek."

It was true, I thought. Everything that I'd learned from *Ideal Marriage,* all its sexual advice and techniques, meant little without love.

I felt sad and alone. I had no girl I loved and who loved me back. No Jessica for me, like Pam for Brian.

I flipped back to the beginning of *Ideal Marriage.* On page 2, it said that a doctor "must risk *all* in order to improve human prospects and potentialities of enduring happiness in marriage."

"The potentialities of enduring happiness in marriage." The idea touched me again, as it had on my first reading it almost two years earlier. As I went on re-reading *Ideal Marriage*, I felt my mood lifting. I wouldn't give up. Making as good a marriage as possible still seemed to me the key to a happy life.

I took out my last letter from Jessica, the one in which she had broken off with me.

"Maybe I feel too young and scared to get involved in something so deep as I know it would be between you and me," she had written. Well, it was a year and a month later now. Jessica might feel less scared. Maybe she'd be ready to see that she *had* thrown away "something that could be really good."

I was a year and a month older, too, and more experienced. Now I might find the right way to reach out to Jessica and get her to see that I would be good for her.

Not because I was so terrific, I told myself, feeling modest, but because of the way in which I would love her, always putting her happiness and welfare ahead of my own.

I recalled the time I had gone down on Gloria, risking humiliation and turning defeat into victory. Why be any less daring now in pursuing what might be my best chance ever for happiness in life?

I decided to write to Jessica again. At first I would just reestablish contact. Then in future letters, I would go slowly, never pressing her, just patiently trying to win her back. If she eventually returned to me, it would be wonderful. If not, I would keep on looking until I found another girl that I loved enough to marry and who felt the same way about me.

Meanwhile, I looked forward to my summer at Bloomingdale's. Every day would bring new crowds of women streaming into the store. And where better to meet them than in my pillow alcove, where their thoughts were already on bed and I was helping them to make their selections?

In fact, I thought, working at Bloomingdale's and loving Jessica would each reinforce the other. The prospect of meeting new women at Bloomingdale's would give me the patience I needed to win Jessica back. And the knowledge that I was trying to win her back would let me enjoy each day at Bloomingdale's without feeling that I was renouncing my ultimate goal. Unlike in Frost's poem, I would be one traveler, but would travel both roads simultaneously.

I took out my block of stationary, pushed away any sadness at the unlikelihood of success, and began to write:

Dear Jessica,
    This may seem strange to you, coming out of the blue....

The End